The Happy Hollisters and the Mystery at Missile Town

BY JERRY WEST

Illustrated by Helen S. Hamilton

GARDEN CITY, N.Y.

Doubleday & Company, Inc.

Contents

1. Countdown!   11
2. Cape Canaveral Dog   20
3. The Missile Monkey   33
4. Tit for Tat   45
5. A Monkey Search   53
6. Tiny Footprints   63
7. A Mysterious Voice   72
8. Congratulations to Pete   79
9. A Trick   87
10. Forbidden Territory   99
11. An Underground Rocket   110
12. Snap the Whip   120
13. A Suspicious Stranger   130
14. Tracking a Faker   139
15. The Funny Warning   149
16. A Strange Catch   157
17. Shadowed   167
18. Young Heroes   176

THE HAPPY HOLLISTERS
AND THE MYSTERY AT MISSILE TOWN

CHAPTER 1

COUNTDOWN!

RICKY Hollister sat in a cone-shaped, wooden object marked "Explorer X," nailed to the top of a six-foot pole. It stood near the garage of the Hollister home. Stationed at various spots nearby were his brother and two sisters.

"Moon rocket man! Are you ready?" Pete called.

The clear July morning made this a perfect day for a missile launching.

"Okay."

"Tracking station?"

"All set!" sang out Pam from the roof of the garage.

"Then start the countdown, Holly," Pete ordered.

The Hollister children's missile game was about to begin, with red-haired, seven-year-old Ricky as the astronaut. On his head was a space helmet which covered half his face. His eyes sparkled as he grinned down at twelve-year-old Pete, crouched behind a sandbox.

Pete, a husky blond boy, held an old radio in one hand. With the other he twisted the dials left and right.

Next to him sat Holly, a six-year-old tomboy with

pigtails. She glanced up at golden-haired Pam, who was ten.

"T minus ten minutes," Holly chirped, looking at her wrist watch.

"Hey! Hold it!" an outsider's voice suddenly demanded. "What's going on here?"

Joey Brill and Will Wilson, twelve-year-old pals, strode into the yard.

"Uh-uh! Trouble!" Pete whispered to Holly. "Hold the countdown!"

Joey Brill, unpopular with the Hollisters because of his many mean tricks, wore a scowl most of the time. Will, a slender boy, usually tagged along after his huskier friend.

"What kind of a sissy game is this?" Joey asked.

"We're playing Cape Canaveral," Pete answered, rising.

"Why are girls in it?" Joey questioned. "Only men launch missiles."

"That shows how much you know!" Ricky called down from his high perch. "Plenty of women have jobs at the missile range. Our Uncle Walt, who works there, said so."

Pete explained that their uncle was in charge of installing the pay load, which was often shot into outer space in the nose cone of rockets.

"It's a very important job, and we're proud of him," Holly added.

"I'm going to be an astronaut some day," Ricky said, lifting his helmet.

"An aster-nut, ha, ha!" Joey laughed. "You're a nut, all right, to be fooling around with silly stuff like this." He walked over and kicked the pole, sending a quiver up to the "missile" in which freckle-nosed Ricky sat.

"Stop that!" Pete ordered. He advanced toward Joey, at the same time keeping an eye on Will.

"Okay. We don't want to play your jerky old game, anyway. Come on, Will."

Joey gave the pole an extra kick, then ran off, with his pal following. They dashed out the driveway and disappeared down the street.

"I hope those pests don't come back," Holly said, breathing a sigh of relief.

From his seat in the nose of the make-believe rocket, Ricky glanced about the "launching site." To him the white, rambling Hollister home on the shore of Pine Lake was the Central Control Building. The glistening body of water was the Atlantic Ocean, and the rowboat tied to the Hollisters' dock was a crash boat, ready to make any necessary rescue.

Pete had squatted into place again beside the sand-box and was turning the radio dials once more. "How's everything down range?" he asked Pam.

His sister scanned the lake with her field glasses. "Weather good. Clouds parting. Resume opera-tions."

"T minus nine minutes," Holly said, and Ricky adjusted the space helmet more securely, awaiting the lift-off.

Holly's eyes were glued to the sweep hand on her watch. "T minus eight—seven—six—five—four—three . . ."

Earlier the Hollisters had practiced making a roaring sound when the lift-off took place. They were all set as the countdown neared zero.

"Two! One!" Holly went on, her voice rising with excitement.

Just then the back door of their home burst open and a little dark-haired girl raced out.

"Pete! Pam! Ricky! Holly!" she cried. "Come into the house quick!"

"Hold the shot!" Pete commanded his rocket crew. "Sue, you spoiled our launching."

Sue paid no attention. She raced across the lawn as fast as her chubby legs could travel. At four, she was the youngest of the children and fondly loved by them all.

The little girl dashed to Pete's side, then tugged him by the hand. "Come on, everybody!"

"Has something happened?" Pete asked.

"You'll see. It's a secret."

"Hey," Ricky called, "I want to hear it too!"

"Me three!" Pam declared. She inched toward the edge of the sloping roof and scrambled down the ladder by which she had reached her watching post.

Meanwhile, Ricky had shinned down the pole. Together the five children raced for the house. They found their mother, a slender, pretty woman with a

The countdown neared zero.

happy smile, seated on the living-room couch, an open letter in her hands.

"What's so important about a letter?" Ricky asked Sue, rather disappointed.

"It's from Aunt Carol," the little girl replied, "and it came extra-special-delivery air mail. Didn't it, Mommy?" Without waiting for a reply Sue continued to bubble, "And on the back Randy and Sharon wrote SWAK."

Pam smiled at her little sister, for she too abbreviated "Sealed with a Kiss" on the letters she wrote to her cousins in Florida.

As the children crowded about, Mrs. Hollister unfolded the letter from her sister, Mrs. Davis. Inside it was a photograph.

"Is it a picture of Sharon and Randy?" asked Holly, standing on tiptoe to look over Ricky's shoulder.

"No," Mrs. Hollister replied and held the picture for the children to see.

It was the photo of a small monkey!

"How cute!"

"Who is she?"

"Is she a new pet?"

Mrs. Hollister read from the back of the picture: "This is Lady Rhesus, who once was shot into outer space."

"Yikes!" Ricky exclaimed. "Who owns her?"

"I'll read you the letter," his mother said, her eyes twinkling.

"Dear Elaine, John, and Children,

"How about paying us a visit? The sooner, the better. We'd love to see you all.

"I know you would enjoy watching the great missile launched, and you children should love playing with Lady Rhesus. I am enclosing her picture. She has been retired from trips to outer space and is now the pet of Miss Mott, a friend of mine.

"Walter and I send our love, as do Sharon and Randy.

Aunt Carol"

"How exciting!" exclaimed Pam.

"Crickets! A trip to Cape Canaveral!" Pete shouted.

"We just *must* go," Holly said, throwing her arms about her mother's neck. "I want to play with Lady Rhesus."

"And I want to see a real rocket fly to the moon," Ricky added.

"There are many things to be considered before we can make the trip," Mrs. Hollister said.

"Like who'll take care of our pets?" Pam asked.

The Happy Hollisters had a collie dog named Zip; a mother cat, White Nose, with five cuddly kittens; and a burro called Domingo. He stayed in a stall in the garage.

"If we do go, when will it be?" Pam asked.

"Your father and I will have to discuss it," her mother replied. "Perhaps——"

17

Mrs. Hollister stopped speaking as a loud braying noise came from the garage.

"That's Domingo," Pete said, stepping toward the door. The burro often did this when someone walked into the garage.

"I'll bet Joey's here again!" Ricky cried out.

He and Pete ran into the yard and glanced around. Nobody was in sight. When the brothers looked in the garage, Domingo tossed his head and brayed again.

"What's the matter, old boy?" Pete stroked the pet. "Did somebody come in here?"

The burro pawed the straw beneath his hoofs. Pete gave him a handful of grain and said, "Thanks for the warning. No damage done by whoever was here."

By this time the other children had come out of the house. They were full of talk about the trip to Cape Canaveral.

"But I still want to pretend to be an astronaut," Ricky said. "Let's finish our game."

"Climb up!" Pete directed. "Everyone take his place!"

The children hurried to their positions and Holly started the countdown again at T minus ten seconds. Finally she called, "*Zero!*"

Instantly the Hollisters gave loud rumbling sounds. Sue clapped her hands. "There goes the rocket!" she cried out.

"Up—up—up through the clouds!" Holly said jubilantly.

For a moment Ricky became so carried away by the game that he stood up and waved to the others. But as he did, the "missile" suddenly teetered.

"Look out!" Pete warned.

There was a tearing, ripping sound as the wooden cone snapped off the six-foot pole. Ricky, tossed out, fell to the ground!

CHAPTER 2

CAPE CANAVERAL DOG

"Oh!" Pam cried out, as her brother lay stunned on the ground.

Pete and Holly ran to Ricky's side, fearful that he was badly injured. Pam fairly flew down the ladder and raced to help him, while Sue dashed into the house, calling her mother.

"Ricky! Ricky! Are you all right?" Holly cried excitedly.

The boy's eyelids fluttered open. "Yikes! I saw stars and thought I was in outer space!" he mumbled.

Just then Mrs. Hollister ran from the house. She asked if Ricky had hit his head and was relieved to learn he had fallen on one shoulder.

Ricky sat up and gave a sickly grin. "I'm okay," he said. "But I didn't reach the moon."

"That might have been a very bad accident," Mrs. Hollister said with concern. "Pete, I thought you said the cone was nailed on tightly."

"It was. I'm going up there to see what happened."

Pete examined the smashed "missile." There were no nails in it. He placed the ladder against the pole and climbed to the top. An hour before, he had nailed the cone securely with three long nails. Now he found only one of them still in the wood!

"Here's the trouble!" Pete called down. "Somebody pulled out two of the nails."

"Wonder who could have done that?" Mrs. Hollister asked. Then, remembering she had to check a pie in the oven, she returned to the house.

As she left, Joey Brill and Will Wilson sauntered into the yard. "What's the matter?" Joey remarked. "Have an accident?"

"Ricky fell out of the rocket," Holly replied.

"That's too bad," Will said. He laughed. "So your rocket shot failed."

"I guess that junky invention of yours wasn't strong enough," Joey added. As he bent over to pick up a piece of the cone, one of his trousers pockets gapped open. Inside were two long nails!

"Oh!" Pam gasped. "You sabotaged our rocket!"

"What do you mean?" Joey glared defiantly at the girl.

"The missing nails are in your pocket."

Joey's face became red. "Prove it!" he blurted.

Pete, who had rushed down the ladder, instantly made a grab for the boy and thrust his left hand into Joey's pocket. As the bully wrenched free, Pete withdrew the nails. "There's the proof!" he shouted.

"Smart guy!" Joey cried, and swung his fist hard.

Pete ducked, then returned Joey a solid punch to the chin.

"Ouch!" Joey cried and backed off. "You hit me when I wasn't looking! I'll get even with you for this!" He and Will ran out of the yard and down the street.

Late that afternoon Mr. Hollister drove home in his station wagon from The Trading Post. This was a combination hardware, toy, and sports shop which he owned in downtown Shoreham.

Holly, waiting for him, raced toward the car.

"Daddy, Daddy! May we go to see the missile monkey?" she asked excitedly.

Her father stepped out, caught the little girl in his arms, and swung her about. He was a tall, athletic-looking man with dark hair and twinkling eyes.

"What's that you say, Pigtails?" he asked, with a wink at Pete and Pam, who had also hurried outside.

"Oh, Mother has told you already," Pam said.

"Indeed she has," Mr. Hollister replied, walking into the house. "You really want to go?"

"Oh, yes!"

During supper the children chattered about the invitation to visit their aunt and uncle. Finally, as they all started to eat generous portions of deep-dish apple pie, Pam said, "Dad, you haven't said yes."

Mr. Hollister looked directly at his wife. "Elaine," he began, smiling, "we are in the age of rockets. I'm afraid these junior astronauts won't be satisfied until they have visited Missile Town, U.S.A."

"I'd love to take them," his wife replied. "It will

be so nice to see Walter, Carol, and the two children."

"Yes," Holly said. With a giggle, she added, "We haven't seen our cousins in a hundred years!"

"It was only five years ago, silly," Pam told her.

"I remember," Sue spoke up.

"You weren't even born then," Ricky told his little sister.

"I was just an angel flying around, wasn't I, Mother?" Sue asked.

Mrs. Hollister smiled.

"Did you see any missiles up there in angel land, Sue?" Ricky continued to tease his little sister.

"Enough of that nonsense," their mother interrupted. She turned to her husband and added, "John, when can you get away?"

Mr. Hollister sighed. "I can't leave town now—too busy. But I want the rest of you to go."

"Oh, Dad, you're wonderful!" Pam exclaimed.

All the children thanked him profusely and said how sorry they were he could not accompany them.

The next few days the Hollister home was a place of hustle and bustle, as preparations for the trip went on. The travelers would go by train and be met by the Davises.

"Boy, we have a lot of stuff to lug with us," Pete remarked, as he watched his mother pack the suitcases.

"If there is anything extra you might like to take, son, speak up now," Mrs. Hollister said.

"I have the extras all ready, Mother." Pete grinned.

He hastened to his room and returned with a large suitcase. Inside were rubber flippers, underwater masks, and snorkel outfits for the five children.

Next day, when everything was set, Mr. Hollister drove his family to the station.

"Don't forget to feed White Nose and the kittens," Holly said as they reached the railroad and got out.

"And see that Zip has fresh water every day," Sue remarked, picking up her midget-sized suitcase for toys.

"And please close the garage doors at night," Pete suggested, "so that Joey Brill won't annoy Domingo."

Mr. Hollister grinned. "Can you think of anything else I have to do, Elaine?" he said.

"Be sure to eat three good meals a day," she said and kissed her husband good-by.

By this time a redcap had all the suitcases on his small truck and wheeled them to the front of the platform. The train came into the station and the luggage was loaded aboard. The five children hugged and kissed their father and stepped onto the train with Mrs. Hollister.

"Don't let Ricky get onto a real rocket by mistake and go to Mars," Mr. Hollister said with a chuckle as the train pulled away. "Have fun, everyone!"

They found their seats in the Pullman car; Ricky and Holly together, with Mrs. Hollister and Sue facing them. Pete and Pam, across the aisle, settled back to study the timetable.

"Where do we get off?" Pam asked her brother.

"At this place," Pete replied, running his finger down the list of towns. "The station is called Cocoa Rockledge. It's on the Indian River."

About four o'clock the train pulled into Washington, D.C. As the travelers peered from the windows the porter stopped to speak to them.

"You'll have time to go outside and walk around," he said. "We're having brake trouble in one of the cars, so there'll be an hour's delay."

"Oh, good!" Pam exclaimed. "Let's take a look at the Capitol dome."

"I'm thirsty," said Sue, tugging at her mother's hand. "May I please have a drink?"

"Certainly, darling." Mrs. Hollister led the children to a drinking fountain and held Sue up to the bubbling water, while the other children waited to drink some too.

"Thank you, Mommy," Sue said, and ran over to sit on a nearby bench.

After Pam, Pete, and Ricky had taken turns drinking the cool water, Mrs. Hollister looked around for Holly. She was nowhere to be seen.

"Where did Holly go?" her mother asked the older children. They did not know.

"Oh, dear!" Mrs. Hollister said nervously. "We must find her quickly."

Pete snapped his fingers. "I have it, Mother. I'll have her paged over the loudspeaker."

Pete hastened across the station to the information desk and told a woman clerk about his sister's disappearance. The woman picked up a microphone, and soon the station resounded with the words: "Will Holly Hollister please return to her family at the drinking fountain?"

"Thank you," Pete said, and raced back to his mother.

"That should bring her," Mrs. Hollister said, smiling.

But Holly did not appear. Just then Sue, who had heard the announcement, skipped to her mother's side. "Are you looking for Holly?"

"Yes. Do you know where she is?"

"Holly's gone to see the President."

"Oh, no!"

"She went out that door," Sue said, pointing. "But don't worry, Mommy. Holly said she'll come back soon."

Holly Hollister, meanwhile, had passed through the main entrance and stood on the sidewalk, watching the taxis whizzing past. The Capitol, she saw, was some distance ahead. She would have to get there and back as quickly as possible if she hoped to see the President before their train departed.

Holly turned left until she came to a crossing. Waiting until the light became green, the little girl turned right across the street, and ran toward the Capitol. Coming finally to a large building, she thought it was the right one and turned in.

But how'll I find the President? Holly wondered.

As she paused, a good-looking man carrying a brief case said, "Hello there. Are you looking for someone?"

"Yes," Holly replied. "In the Capitol."

The man smiled down on the pigtailed girl. "That's the next building, but take the underground train. You'll like it. The train goes straight to the Capitol."

"Thank you," Holly said. The man showed her to the tracks, then said good-by.

Holly found herself in a white, shiny tunnel. Beside the tracks stood a long, glistening vehicle which reminded her of an open roller-coaster car. People were stepping onto it. Holly followed and sat between a man and a woman, who smiled at her as the car started.

"This is fun," Holly said, hunching her shoulders and giggling softly.

"Yes, it is," the woman replied. She looked about the car and asked, "Are your parents with you?"

"Oh, no," Holly said. "Mommy's at the station."

The woman looked disturbed and spoke to the man. "Is this little girl with you?"

"No, madam. I thought she was yours." He looked straight at Holly and added, "Where are you going, little miss?"

"*I'm looking for the President.*"

"To see the President."

"I'm sorry," said the man, "but the President is out of town. He won't be back for several weeks."

"Oh!" Holly said, disappointed, as the car came to a halt beneath the Capitol.

"Does your mother know where you are?" the woman asked.

"No. But Sue does. She'll tell her."

As the other passengers got off, the woman put an arm about Holly's shoulders. "I'm a Senator," she said sweetly, "but my business can wait until I return you to your family."

"Thank you," Holly said, fidgeting with a pigtail. "I hope my mother isn't worrying about me."

The little car returned to the building from where it had started. As Holly and the lady Senator stepped off, a policeman rushed to the platform, followed by Mrs. Hollister and the rest of the children.

"There she is! Thank goodness!" Mrs. Hollister said as she flung her arms about the missing girl.

"This lady brought me back," Holly said, "'cause the President isn't home."

Mrs. Hollister thanked the woman, and told how they had questioned passers-by all along the street until they had discovered the route Holly had taken.

"You must never go off in a strange city again," Mrs. Hollister said. She glanced at her watch. "The train leaves in ten minutes. If we race back, we may catch it."

The Hollisters hurried outside, beckoned to a cab

driver, and asked to go to the station. They reached their train just as the conductor was calling, "All aboard!"

"Oh, I'm glad we made it," said Holly, who was very ashamed of her escapade.

The children enjoyed supper in the diner. When they returned to their Pullman, they saw that their seats had been made into beds, and there were others above them.

"You boys will sleep in the upper berth," Mrs. Hollister said, and her sons climbed up. "Pete on the outside, please, and don't fall out!"

During the night the locomotive roared along, pulling the great line of cars through the southern states. By the time the Hollisters were seated in the dining car next morning, the countryside looked very different to the children from that around Shoreham. Pinewoods and quaint little towns zipped past the wide windows.

A few hours later, when the sun was directly over-head, the porter came to say, "Next stop, Cocoa-Rockledge!"

"I hope Aunt Carol and Sharon and Randy meet us," Pam said. "Oh, I can hardly wait to see them!"

"I want to see a missile go up right away," Ricky announced.

The train slowed, finally coming to a stop. The Hollisters, standing near the door, looked out at a tiny wooden station. When they stepped down to it,

Pam's eyes swept the platform for a sight of their relatives.

"Here they come!" she cried out, pointing to a station wagon that had just driven up.

Both front doors opened. A boy and a girl climbed out one side, and a pretty woman with reddish golden hair out the other.

"Sharon! Randy! Aunt Carol!" The Hollister children rushed forward with kisses for their aunt and girl cousin. Randy received hearty backslaps.

Mrs. Hollister embraced her sister, then her niece and nephew. Sharon, eleven, looked very much like her cousin Pam. Randy, eight, was dark-haired and had mischievous dark eyes.

"Where's Lady Rhesus?" Sue asked, tugging at Aunt Carol.

"At Miss Mott's home. We'll see the monkey later."

Suddenly Sharon said to Randy, "Where's Missy?"

"In the back of the car. I'll get her."

Randy returned a few seconds later, holding a dachshund in his arms. "This is Missy," he said. "That's short for Missile."

He set the dog on the ground and Pam leaned down to pat her. Missy started to shiver. "Oh, she's scared," Pam said sympathetically.

"No, it's not that," Sharon said with a grin.

Missy began to whine. The Hollister children

31

looked concerned, but their cousins began to laugh. Then they shouted:

"Missile! Missile! Look!"

The startled visitors gazed into the eastern sky but saw nothing.

"Keep looking!" Randy said.

"I see it!" Ricky cried out.

A slender missile, fire streaming from its tail, rose majestically into the blue sky.

"Oh!" Pam cried. "Isn't it marvelous!"

Now the watchers could hear a great rumbling sound in the distance like the passing of a hundred freight trains. The missile continued to rise straight up. But as the rocket began to arch toward the southeast there came a sudden blinding flash and billows of white smoke.

The missile exploded into thousands of pieces!

Everyone gasped, and Randy cried out, "There goes poor Thuzzy!"

Sharon's lips quivered. She burst out crying.

"Come now," Aunt Carol said, wiping the girl's tears away. "I'm sure the next bird will be successful."

"Thuzzy? Bird?" Pete asked. "What is all this about?"

CHAPTER 3

THE MISSILE MONKEY

"THUZZY," Aunt Carol explained, "is short for your Uncle Walt's pet expression for a missile. He calls them all Thuzzenelda."

The children giggled, although Pam said it was a shame that the missile which had just been launched had been a failure.

Her next question was how had Missy known that the rocket was about to go off.

Sharon answered. "She was born on the base at Cape Canaveral. Missy has extra-sensitive hearing, like all dogs, so she knows when a rocket's going off even before human beings do. It gets her excited. That's why she shakes and whimpers."

"Don't you own her?" Pete asked.

"Sure we do," Randy answered. "The man who had her was transferred from this base to one in California. He gave Missy to us."

Sue clapped her hands. "I love it here. I can play with the Carnival dog and monkey."

"Can-av-er-al," Pam corrected her.

The cousins loaded the baggage into the back of the station wagon and they all climbed in. Mrs. Hollister and her sister sat in front, with Sue on her mother's lap.

"What's a bird?" Pam asked Randy as they drove along.

"Oh, that's what everybody around here calls the missiles," he replied.

"Do you want to hear something funny?" Sharon said. "When a missile firing is canceled, the missile men say that they have 'scrubbed a bird.'"

"That is funny," Holly agreed.

Mrs. Hollister smiled. "Once, when Pete was a little boy," she said, "we had a canary. When Pete gave him a bath, he actually scrubbed the poor bird."

"Was he canceled, Mummy?" Sue chirped.

"The poor bird nearly was," her mother replied, "but fortunately he did recover."

"I remember that," said Pete. "Boy, was I scared!"

The Hollisters learned that the railroad station was on the outskirts of the town of Cocoa, where the Davises lived. Aunt Carol drove to the center of the city, then made a right-hand turn toward the residential section. It was situated on a wide body of water.

"This is the Indian River," Sharon told her cousins.

"I've seen that name on oranges we get up North," Pam recalled.

Soon Aunt Carol drove up alongside a large, one-story ranch-type house. Two tall palm trees grew in front of it and many flowering bushes decorated the property. On one side of the house towered a tall, gaunt oak tree, its branches draped with thick gray moss.

"Our home," said Aunt Carol. "Welcome, everybody!"

"This place is swell!" Pete said admiringly.

After the bags had been carried into the house, the Davises showed the guests to their bedrooms. Ricky and Pete were to sleep in Randy's room. It contained a single bed and double-decker bunks.

"Yikes! May I have the top bunk?" Ricky asked, climbing to the upper bed with the agility of a monkey.

"Okay with me," Pete said, "only don't fall out in the middle of the night."

"I didn't on the train," the younger boy defended himself.

Sharon in the meantime had led her girl cousins into her room. The walls were painted pink, and white ruffled curtains hung at the windows. In the room were twin beds and two smaller folding cots, which Sharon said were for Holly and Sue.

Pam glanced out the window. "This is going to be great fun, Sharon," she said, noting that the property extended right to the waterfront. "What a lovely dock you have."

"Do the boys like to fish?" Sharon asked.

"Oh, sure," Holly answered. "And so do I."

Sue stood on tiptoes to look out another window. "Oh, Pam, come here!"

"What is it?"

"A lady riding a bicycle with a monkey on her back."

"That's Miss Mott and Lady Rhesus," Sharon said. The girls ran into the living room and out the front door to meet her.

Miss Mott was a middle-aged woman, whose black hair was turning gray. She wore it in a perky ponytail, which made her look much younger. On her shoulders sat a tiny monkey.

"Hello, Sharon," she said gaily, parking her bicycle at the curb and walking toward the house.

"Miss Mott," Sharon said, "I'd like you to meet my cousins." And she introduced them.

The girls politely said, "How do you do," but they could not keep their eyes off the tiny monkey. Her hands moved quickly this way and that, as if she were trying to hide her face from the children's stares.

"And this is Lady Rhesus, the space monkey," Miss Mott said as they walked toward the house. "I helped train her for the missile test, and when it was over, got her back again."

"I think she's adorable," Pam said. With that, the monkey jumped from her owner's shoulder and landed on the girl's.

"Eek!" Pam exclaimed, and held her neck stiffly.

"Don't worry," Miss Mott said. "Lady Rhesus will not hurt you. In fact, you're honored to have her jump on your shoulder. That proves she likes you."

Pam took the monkey off her shoulder and carried her inside the house. The group entered the living room just as the boys came from their bedroom.

"And this is Lady Rhesus, the space monkey."

"Yikes!" Ricky said. "Where did you get the monkey, Pam?"

Before answering, she introduced Miss Mott to her family. Then the children got Lady Rhesus to play with them.

"She's very entertaining," Miss Mott said, and told the monkey to play circus.

Obediently Lady Rhesus did a handspring, then a somersault. Finally she lay down with her arms spread out.

"Now Lady's pretending to be in the missile," her owner explained. "She was strapped down and various instruments were clamped to her body."

As the Hollisters gazed at the monkey, Sue suddenly said, "I know how to somersault!" With that she got down on the floor and flipped her feet over her head.

Crash!

Everyone turned just in time to see the television set teetering. Pete made a leap and steadied the instrument. As Sue arose, looking very frightened, music suddenly began to play and a dancer showed on the screen. Everyone laughed.

"You're quite a circus performer yourself, Sue," said Aunt Carol.

The only one who did not think the accident funny was Lady Rhesus. Frightened by the commotion, she had leaped to Miss Mott's shoulder and was hugging her mistress tightly.

"I'm terribly sorry 'bout everything," Sue said to the monkey and to Aunt Carol.

"No harm done," her aunt said, smiling.

"I must go now," Miss Mott spoke up. "I just came to tell you, Carol, about our art-club meeting. It has been postponed." She turned to the Hollister children. "I live on the Banana River. There's very good fishing. I have a boat, and if you should want to borrow it sometime, let me know."

"Thank you," Pete said. "I'd sure like to do that."

Ricky grinned. "I know why you live on the Banana River, Miss Mott," he said. "So Lady Rhesus can have plenty of bananas to eat!"

Everybody laughed, as Miss Mott said good-by. With the monkey on her shoulder she rode off down the street.

Shortly afterward Uncle Walt Davis arrived from work and parked his small car in the drive.

"Hey, Daddy!" Randy called out. "They're here!"

Uncle Walt was shorter than their father. He was a slender, square-jawed man, and his mouth turned up at the corners. Right now, however, he looked tired and disappointed. He exchanged greetings with the relatives and said how happy he was they had come to Florida.

"We saw Thuzzy blow up," Ricky said. "That was a shame."

"It was a big disappointment," his uncle admitted.

"What caused it to explode?" Pete asked.

"No one knows," Uncle Walt replied, "but we're trying to find out."

He said that the missile had lifted off the launching pad perfectly, but something had gone wrong just as the bird was about to fly down the Atlantic Missile Range.

"When all the pieces are picked up, I suppose we'll know the answer to the riddle," he added. "The pay load cost three million dollars to build, so we're eager to locate it."

"So you can use it again?" Pete asked.

"Not that so much," the missile man replied, "but we don't want it to get into the wrong hands."

"Like foreign spies?" Ricky asked excitedly.

"Something like that," Uncle Walt replied, smiling.

"Then we'll help you find it!" Holly offered.

"That will be fine." Uncle Walt explained that the debris had fallen partly near the beaches and partly in the ocean.

"We'll go looking for the pieces right away," Randy said.

Aunt Carol smiled at her young son's enthusiasm but said that dinner was ready. She suggested they start their sleuthing first thing in the morning.

Pete and Ricky were interested in their uncle's little car, which was a sedan of foreign make and held only four passengers. Randy and his sister referred to it as the Bug.

"May we go for a ride in the Bug?" Ricky asked his uncle.

"Tomorrow, yes. If you three boys hunt for missile debris I'll drive you over to Cocoa Beach on my way to work tomorrow morning."

The next day was bright and sunny. After breakfast the three boys waved good-by to the others and piled into the Bug. Soon Uncle Walt was driving them across a long causeway, across Merritt Island, toward the long beach, on one end of which was located the Cape Canaveral firing range.

Randy explained to his cousins that the beach extended far into the south. "Patrick is located at the other end," he said.

"Patrick who?" Ricky asked.

Randy laughed. "Patrick Air Force Base."

Uncle Walt explained that this place housed the administrative end of the missile base. "The executive offices and laboratories are located there," he said. "Also an airport."

When they reached Cocoa Beach, Uncle Walt let the three boys off and gave his son some money with which to buy lunch.

"Aunt Carol will call for you this afternoon," he told Pete. "Be at this end of the beach about three o'clock."

Pete and Ricky thanked their uncle, and hurried to the seashore, where the waves gently lapped the wide sandy beach. The Hollister boys noticed that cars were being driven back and forth across the finely packed sand.

"Yikes, this is keen!" Ricky said. "Do you suppose we can do that sometime, Randy?"

"Sure. Everybody does."

As the boys started walking along the beach they could see other people looking here and there for debris from the exploded missile.

"I hope we find something," Pete said, searching among the sea shells washed up by the waves. "It would be neat, Randy, to help your dad find out why that bird exploded."

Soon a fourth boy, walking barefoot in the sand, approached them. "Hey, Randy!" he called from a distance. "Who are those two kids with you?"

Randy whispered to his cousins, "That's Marshall Holt. We call him Marsh. He's a pain. Lives down the beach aways."

When Marshall ran up to the three boys, Pete sized him up. He was a heavyset blond lad, about thirteen years old, and wore a scowl.

"Hello, Marsh," Randy said. "Meet my cousins, Pete and Ricky Hollister, from up North."

"Howdy," Marsh replied, glancing down the beach. "Everybody's hunting for pieces of the rocket. I suppose you are too."

"That's right," Randy replied.

"Had any luck?"

"No, we just got here."

"Well, if you find anything, let me know."

"Why?" Pete asked.

"So I can take it to Patrick," Marsh said. "All the kids around here are going to report to me."

"Well, we're not," Randy said.

"You don't have to act smart," Marsh declared sharply, "just because your cousins are with you. Well, remember what I said." He hurried along the beach, his eyes fixed on the sand.

"Marsh is a pest," Randy remarked. "He always wants to be the boss of everything."

"Like Joey Brill in our town," Pete added.

After the boys had walked for a mile along the water's edge they headed toward the low dunes which bordered the beach. Thick tufts of coarse grass grew here and there on them. Bits of driftwood were scattered on sandy spots where picnickers had built bonfires.

Ricky kicked at several pieces of the wood. Suddenly his toe hit something hard and shiny. "Hey, Pete, look at this!" he cried out.

Dropping to his knees, Ricky cupped the sand from around the shiny piece of metal and pulled it out.

His brother laughed. "It's only an old hubcap."

At the same time Marsh ran toward them, waving his arms. He arrived breathless. "What have you got there? Give it to me!"

"I won't," Ricky replied, holding the hubcap behind his back.

"It's nothing anyway," Pete said with a chuckle.

"I don't believe you."

"Show him, Ricky."

When the red-haired boy held the hubcap toward Marsh, his face flushed with embarrassment and anger.

"Oh, trying to play a big joke on me, eh?" With that he slapped the hubcap from Ricky's hand so hard that it banged the younger boy's foot painfully.

"Ow!" Ricky cried, and danced around on one leg.

"You have some nerve, Marsh!" Pete said hotly.

"I don't like you," came the reply, and Marsh shoved Pete backward in the sand.

Instantly Pete sprang to his feet, clenching his fists. But Marsh had turned and was running across the beach. Pete went after the bully, Ricky and Randy at his heels. They raced around a dune, behind which an old weather-beaten shack stood in the shade of some dilapidated palm trees. Behind the shack was a rutted lane which cut through a thicket of scrubby pines. When Pete reached it, Marsh was out of sight.

Just then the back door of the shack opened and a gaunt, craggy-browed man stepped out. He wore dark trousers and a faded blue shirt which matched the color of his squinty eyes.

"Get away from here!" he thundered.

"I'm sorry," Pete said. "We want——"

"I said scram!" The man sprang forward and shook his fist.

CHAPTER 4

TIT FOR TAT

FRIGHTENED by the gruff man, Pete, Ricky, and Randy turned and ran to the beach. Finally they stopped and looked back. The stranger had gone inside the shack and closed the door.

"Yikes!" Ricky exclaimed. "I thought he was going to hurt us."

"He sure was mad," Pete said. "Who is he, Randy?"

"I never saw him before."

The three boys continued along the beach, looking for missile parts. In the distance a low car approached, with a large white figure decorating the hood.

"What's that?" Pete asked. As the car came closer, he shielded his eyes from the bright sunlight.

"It's a jeep with a white dog standing on it!" Randy declared.

The children laughed at the strange sight of a dog standing like a statue on the flat hood. The driver slowed up and stopped beside the boys. He was a friendly-looking man, wearing tan dungarees and a white T shirt. His face and arms were deeply tanned and he sported a bristly gray crew cut.

"Hello, Boys!" he called cheerfully.

"Hi!" Pete replied. "Excuse us for laughing, but we never saw a live dog used as an ornament."

"That's Whitey's favorite place to ride," the man said. "If you've never seen him before, I know you're new to this beach."

Pete introduced himself, Ricky, and Randy, then told of the Hollisters' visit to Florida.

"My name is George Hoffman," the man said, leaning over to shake hands. "But everybody calls me Mr. Jeep."

"Glad to meet you," Pete smiled. "Are you on a vacation?"

Mr. Jeep said that he was a retired police officer who used his spare time towing cars which became mired on the beach. "It's surprising how many get stuck," he explained.

"You must know this area well," Pete said.

"Indeed I do."

"Then maybe you can tell us about the man who lives over there," Pete said, pointing to the shack.

"His name is Alec Ferguson," Mr. Jeep replied. "He's a shrimp fisherman—new to this beach. He doesn't like people to come near his place."

"We found that out!" Ricky declared, and told of their experience.

As they chatted, Whitey remained motionless on the hood of the car, the ocean breeze ruffling his fluffy fur.

"Well, I'm sorry you boys had a bad scare," Mr.

Jeep said. "How would you like a ride to help you forget about it?"

"Great!" Pete said.

"Hop aboard."

Ricky and Randy clambered into the back seat while Pete took his place beside the driver.

"This is great fun!" Pete commented, as they drove mile after mile along the sandy shore. "Look there," he added. "I think someone's in trouble."

A red and white sedan was parked at the edge of the water, and a man stood beside the car, waving his arms.

Mr. Jeep pulled along side and stopped. "What's the trouble?" he asked.

The man said his front wheel had hit a hole in the sand. "The car won't budge, and the tide's coming in," he added worriedly.

Mr. Jeep explained that sometimes children dug holes in the sand and forgot to fill them. "They've trapped a lot of cars that way," he said, stepping out of his automobile. "Come on, fellows, lend a hand."

At his direction, Ricky and Randy pulled a tow-rope from the floor of his car. Pete attached one end to the front axle of the stranded car and the other to the back of the jeep. The ex-policeman's powerful little vehicle moved slowly across the beach, pulling the other car free.

"Thanks!" said the driver gratefully.

"Don't mention it. Next time watch out for holes," Mr. Jeep replied. "Okay, all aboard, boys."

"Come on, fellows, lend a hand."

As they drove back, Pete told about their search for the missile debris.

"I don't think you'll have much luck finding any on the beach," Mr. Jeep said. "This place has been pretty well searched. I suggest you look in the shallow water."

"But how can we see the bottom?" Randy remarked.

Pete snapped his fingers. "We have the answer to that," he said, and told Randy of the skin-diving equipment they had brought from Shoreham.

"With the snorkel and face mask," Ricky said, "we can search in the shallow water."

"And the flippers will help us to swim better, too," Pete added.

Reaching the spot where he had picked up the boys, Mr. Jeep let them off.

"Thanks for the ride," Pete said, as they waved good-by.

The driver waved back. "Good luck, fellows."

"I wish we had the diving stuff right now," Ricky sighed.

The boys continued the hunt on foot without success until three o'clock, when Aunt Carol called for the cousins in her station wagon. When they arrived home, Pete told the girls of their plan to go skin diving.

"May we help too?" Pam asked.

"Sure," said Pete. He went to his room and returned with the suitcase holding the equipment.

49

Aunt Carol suggested that they continue the search after supper. The tide would be going out and the weatherman promised a calm sea that evening.

"But I think"—Mrs. Hollister spoke up—"that Holly and Sue had better stick to the beach."

Uncle Walt telephoned that he was working late, so an early supper was planned for the children. Shortly after six o'clock, their mothers drove with them to Cocoa Beach. The cousins scampered out of the car in their bathing suits and raced toward the water's edge. Sharon and Randy had their own skin-diving outfits. The five children put on their masks and flippers.

"Don't go down too deep," Pete warned Pam and Ricky, "or else water will get into the snorkel."

The five cousins resembled a school of baby whales as, in their search, they swam slowly along the sandy bottom, the flippers kicking up foam behind them.

The children noticed many different kinds of shells, but nothing that looked like debris from the exploded missile. Then suddenly Pete spied someone's foot ahead of him and bumped into the person before the two could stop moving.

Pete stood up quickly and whipped off his mask. He was face to face with Marshall Holt.

"You!" he exclaimed.

"Yes, and what's it to you?" Marsh flared back.

Just then Ricky's head bobbed up. "Oh, it's Marshmallow!" he taunted.

Randy took up the chant. "Marshmallow! Marshmallow!"

Pam giggled but said, "You shouldn't call people names."

"Say, these are neat outfits you have," Marsh said, changing the subject.

"We're using them to look for debris," Pam said politely.

"Oh, I can see the bottom without wearing goggles," the boy bragged, and added, "Come on, I'll show you."

Pam descended beneath the surface and Marshall swam beside her a distance. Then, without warning, he grabbed her face mask and pulled it off. The salt water got into Pam's eyes, nose, and mouth. She choked and struggled to the surface.

"Don't do that again!" Pete cried out as Marsh dropped the mask and ran to the beach. Pete quickly recovered the mask for his sister.

"I was only having fun!" Marsh called. "Can't you take a joke?" The bully kept his distance, however, while the Hollister and Davis children continued their search.

In a few minutes Ricky stood up and beckoned. "Pete, come here. See what I found!" he called in a loud voice.

Marsh, curious, ran into the water again and approached Ricky. "Is it a piece of the missile?" he asked.

Ricky winked at Pete and said, "Oh, boy, it's right down there."

The bully came closer. "Where?"

"Can't you see it?" Ricky said, pointing.

Marsh bent his head close to the water. As he did, Ricky shoved his face under the surface. Marsh came up spluttering and gasping for breath. "I'll get you for this!" he threatened and ran away.

When the sun set, Aunt Carol called the children and they started back home.

"Shucks," Ricky said, "we didn't find a single piece of the missile."

"Keep on and maybe you will," his mother encouraged him.

As the car approached the Davis house, Sue noticed a bicycle standing at the curb. "The monkey lady's here!" she called out.

"Oh, goody, I want to play with Lady Rhesus!" Holly cried.

The children hurried into the house to find Miss Mott talking with Uncle Walt. The friendly monkey was not on her shoulder. Pam thought the artist looked very sad.

"Miss Mott is very upset," Uncle Walt said, rising from his chair, "because Lady Rhesus is lost!"

CHAPTER 5

A MONKEY SEARCH

LADY Rhesus' disappearance came as a great shock to everyone.

"The poor little monkey," Pam said. "Do you think she was stolen?"

"She was playing in the house," Miss Mott said. "The screen door was slightly ajar. Lady might have slipped out."

"Maybe she's hiding nearby," Pete suggested. "Do you have trees on your property, Miss Mott?"

"There is an orange grove not far away."

"Lady Rhesus could be hiding there," Sharon said hopefully.

"Oh, Mommy," cried Sue, with a frightened look in her eyes, "maybe someone took Lady Rhesus to put her in a missile again!"

"I hardly think so," her mother said reassuringly, but still the little girl fretted. "Poor Lady Rhesus!" she said. "I hope they don't shoot her to the moon!"

The cousins volunteered to look for the pet the next day. Miss Mott thanked them and said she must go home before it grew darker.

When she had left, Pete said, "I think I'll phone Mr. Jeep. He knows lots of people and he might be able to find a clue to Lady Rhesus."

He made the call. The retired policeman was at home. "I'll be happy to look for the monkey," he said. "And when I ride up and down the beach tomorrow, I'll ask everyone I meet."

After breakfast next morning, Aunt Carol drove her sister and the children across town to Miss Mott's cottage. Missy joined the Davises, as she often did when they went out in the car.

Miss Mott greeted the visitors and ushered them into a gracious living room.

"Any news of the monkey?" Pam asked.

"No, unfortunately. And I feel very bad about it. I must console myself with my painting," the artist said.

In one corner of the room were several easels on which stood half-completed canvases of ocean scenes.

"These are so pretty," Sharon remarked.

"I love to paint the water," Miss Mott replied. "The colors are beautiful and always changing."

After the boys had glanced at the pictures, they ran outside onto a green lawn which stretched to the shore of the Banana River.

"This river runs right past Cape Canaveral," Randy said, pointing to the north. He added, "We're very close to the place where the missiles are launched."

"Say, where's Missy?" Ricky asked, looking around. "Maybe she can tell us whether another rocket is going up."

The dachshund was not in sight, but as soon as

Randy whistled, the dog ran from around the corner of the house. "How about it," Randy said, "will there be a shoot today?"

Missy looked over the water toward Cape Canaveral and wagged her tail.

"That means no," Randy said. "Sorry, fellows."

"Well," Pete said, "let's look for Lady Rhesus."

They returned to the house to have Miss Mott show them the neighbor's large orange grove. She had obtained permission from the owners for the children to search it.

"Oh, goody!" Holly said. "May we eat the oranges too, Miss Mott?"

"Only the ones you find on the ground," the artist said, smiling.

The women remained at her house, while the children searched with Missy for the lost monkey.

They ran into the grove, which was laid out in neat straight lines. The trees were laden with fruit, and many of the branches were weighted down.

"Lady Rhesus, where are you?" Sharon called out, as she looked up among the heavily leafed branches of the orange trees.

"Please come back," Holly begged.

The children searched tree after tree, but there was no sign of the pet. Sue stopped beneath a tree to pick up a ripe orange, which she peeled and ate.

"Um, this is delicious!" she said. When she had finished it, she picked up another.

"Don't eat too many," Pam warned her.

"But they are full of vitamins. Mommy said so," Sue declared.

The search went on for more than an hour, and the children wearied of their task.

"We've covered the whole grove," Pete said, "and no Lady Rhesus."

On the trek back to Miss Mott's house, Sue was strangely silent. She tagged along behind Pam, a queer expression on her face.

On arriving at the cottage, they found the three women seated on the shaded patio.

"No luck finding Lady Rhesus," Pete said.

"But we'll keep on looking," Holly declared. "We'll find Lady, don't worry, Miss Mott."

When Mrs. Hollister's eyes fell on Sue, she called out in alarm. "What has happened to you, dear?"

Sue tried to smile, but only one corner of her mouth turned up.

"Don't you feel well?" Aunt Carol asked.

The little girl's black bobbed hair swayed when she nodded. "I'm all right," she said, "but I'm too full of vitamins."

Holly spoke up, "She means all the oranges she ate."

"Goodness," Mrs. Hollister said, "how many did you have?"

Before Sue could answer, Holly spoke up, "I kept count, Mommy. She ate six of them."

"No wonder she looks ill," Mrs. Hollister said,

"We've searched the grove and no Lady Rhesus."

taking the little girl by the hand. "You come inside and lie down until you feel better."

"Take her into my room!" Miss Mott called, and Mrs. Hollister went into the house.

Presently the artist asked the children if they had worked up good appetites. When they said they had, she announced, "Please come inside. I have luncheon prepared for you."

After washing their hands, all the children except Sue and the three women sat down to a table on which were plates of sandwiches and glasses of milk.

"Cricket!" Pete declared. "This sure looks good, Miss Mott."

While they ate, the artist told the visitors something about the area surrounding Cape Canaveral.

"We're in Brevard County," she said. "It has a very interesting history."

"How did Cocoa get its name?" Pam asked. "Were there cocoa trees here?"

"Oh, no," Miss Mott said, smiling. "It is a very funny story."

She told the cousins that the first houses in Cocoa were built in 1881. At that time the place was called Indian River City.

"That's a keen name," Ricky said.

"But it was too long to use as a postmark," Miss Mott went on, "so the U.S. postal authorities decided that the town should change its name.

"About that time a shipment of canned cocoa arrived at the freight station. When someone saw the box with 'Cocoa' written on it, he said, 'How about you all naming this place Cocoa?' And they did."

The Hollister children laughed, then Pete asked, "How did Cape Canaveral get its name?"

Miss Mott told him that *cañaveral* was an old Spanish word meaning "canebrake."

"It was given to the cape by a man named Mendez, the first Spanish governor of Florida."

"Then there must have been sugar cane here," Pam ventured.

"There was, dear. Sugar cane was raised by the large Indian settlement of Ays. They were the first citizens of the cape."

Just then a little voice was heard at the door of Miss Mott's bedroom and Sue padded out. "Mommy, my vitamin tummy ache is all gone. May I have a sandwich?"

Everyone laughed, and Sue was soon seated at the table with the others.

"And there is one more thing you can tell your teachers when you return to Shoreham," Miss Mott continued her story. "Mention of Cape Canaveral was found on maps made in 1574. And Ponce de León knew about this place, too. He used it as a refuge harbor in stormy weather."

Sue had just finished drinking her milk when a knock sounded at the door. Miss Mott went to answer.

"The Hollisters?" the children heard her ask. "Yes, they are here. Won't you come in?"

The door opened and in walked Marshall Holt.

"Marsh!" Randy said, rising from his chair. He introduced his mother and aunt, then said, "How did you know we were here?"

"I met Mr. Jeep on the beach," Marsh replied. "He told me you were looking for a monkey so I rode my bike to the Davises' house."

Aunt Carol smiled and said, "Then you saw the note on the door I had written to my husband telling him we were going to Miss Mott's place."

"Yes," Marsh said, and added, "if you kids are looking for the monkey, she isn't over here."

"What do you mean?" Miss Mott asked. "Do you know where Lady Rhesus is?"

"Of course I do."

"Where?" everyone chorused.

"In that big old mossy oak tree behind the Davis house," he answered.

"Let's go home right away and look!" Sharon suggested eagerly.

After thanking Marshall for his discovery, and Miss Mott for the snack, the children hastened out to the car and drove off with Aunt Carol and Mrs. Hollister.

"We'll phone you if we find Lady," Pam called.

Ten minutes later the cousins stood at the base of the tall oak tree, looking up into its moss-laden branches.

"Lady Rhesus, if you're up there, come down!" Pam coaxed.

But there was no sound or any sight of the little monkey.

"I'll climb up and take a look," Holly volunteered.

Aunt Carol shot a quick glance at her sister. Mrs. Hollister smiled. "It's all right, Carol," she said. "Holly can climb trees like a monkey!"

"And she's small enough to get through some of those tangled branches," Pam added, as she saw Pete and Ricky about to offer.

Pete boosted his sister to a lower limb of the oak tree and Holly scampered up. In a few minutes she was out of sight in the topmost branches.

"Do you see Lady Rhesus?" Sharon asked.

"Not yet," came the reply. Then Holly cried, "I see something! I think it's Lady Rhesus!"

The watchers at the foot of the tree craned their necks to look through the curtain of moss which concealed Holly from view.

"She'll jump on your shoulder if you call to her," Aunt Carol said.

Just then Holly's voice said, "Oh dear, what a mean trick!"

"What happened?" Ricky asked.

"That mean old Marshmallow!" Holly declared. "He stuck a piece of old fur up here just to fool us."

Just then something fell from the tree and landed on the ground. It was an old moth-eaten brown squirrel neckpiece.

"Probably Marsh's mother threw it away," Pam said in disgust. "Why would Marsh go to all that trouble to fool us? Not just because we ducked him in the water!"

"I'm coming down now!" Holly called.

They could hear her carefully stepping down from limb to limb in the descent from the tall tree.

Suddenly the pigtailed girl cried out, "Ugh! This is awful!"

"What's the matter, dear?" Mrs. Hollister asked.

"Mother, I'm all tangled up in this moss and I can't get loose!"

CHAPTER 6

TINY FOOTPRINTS

"HOLD on," Pete called to Holly, "until I get you down!"

"I'll help," Sharon offered.

The two children shinned up to the lowest branch of the oak tree.

"I see her now!" Pete called down to the watchers.

Soon he was on the branch beneath Holly. It was easy to figure out what had happened. A great chunk of gray moss had fallen on top of Holly's head and, in her frantic effort to pull it off, the little girl's arms had become entangled. Pete directed Sharon to climb to one side of Holly while he steadied her on the other.

"Pull all the moss off, while I hold onto her," Pete directed Sharon.

"Thank you," Holly said, not knowing whether to cry or giggle. She climbed down the tree, and her rescuers followed.

On the ground once more, Holly breathed a sigh of relief. "Just wait until I see Marshmallow again!" she said, pursing her lips.

"I think you should stay away from him," Aunt Carol advised. She added quickly, "All of you come into the house. Perhaps a nice cold glass of soda will make you feel better."

Shortly after the children had finished their treat, Uncle Walt drove up in the Bug. Sharon quickly told him of their adventures and asked, "Any good news about Thuzzy?"

Her father shook his head. As yet no one had found a clue as to why the missile had exploded.

"The search for debris has been intensified," Uncle Walt said. "Just about everybody in Brevard County is looking for pieces of the rocket."

"We haven't given up yet," Pete declared.

"I have an idea!" Randy exclaimed. "Let's go on a double hunt tomorrow for the piece of missile and the monkey. We'll make a game of it."

Randy suggested that Pete, Ricky, and Holly search along the beach with snorkels and masks. He, Sharon, Pam, and Sue would continue to look for Lady Rhesus.

"We'll win!" Sue cried out.

Ricky grinned. "Bet you *we* will!"

After supper the telephone rang. Mr. Jeep was calling for Pete.

"Oh, hello," the boy said. "Any news about the monkey?"

"Good news," came the reply. Mr. Jeep reported that a monkey had been seen at Cocoa Beach close to the spot where he had met the boys.

"I can't be sure whether it was Miss Mott's mon-

key or not," he said, "but it might do well to search
the beach around that spot."

Pete thanked Mr. Jeep and hung up. "Say,
Randy," he said excitedly, "this will be great fun.
We can all go to the beach tomorrow and have our
double search there. Some of us will look for the frag-
ment of missile; the rest, for the monkey.

Taking along three skin-diving sets, the cousins
climbed into the station wagon next morning, and
Aunt Carol drove them to Cocoa Beach, promising
to call for them later.

"Okay," Pete said. "Ricky, Holly, and I will look
along the bottom, while the rest of you hunt for Lady
Rhesus."

"How will we do that?" Randy asked.

"Look for footprints," Pam told him.

The Hollister children had played "detective"
many times before. Tracking footprints was one of
the first things a sleuth had to do in searching for a
person or an animal.

"I have another idea," Randy said.

"What?" Pete asked.

A twinkle came into Randy's eyes. "I'll tell you
later, when I get back."

"Where are you going?" his sister demanded.

Randy pointed to a large motel and restaurant
located several hundred yards from the beach front.

"Wait here," he said. "You'll see." He ran off and
disappeared over a dune.

In the meantime the underwater crew put on their

skin-diving equipment, wriggled into their flippers, and walked toward the water's edge. Soon Pete, Ricky, and Holly were breathing through their snorkels and scanning the sandy bottom.

Pam, Sharon, and Sue waited for Randy to return. Five minutes later his head appeared over the dune again and he ran toward them, a brown paper bag held tightly in one hand.

"What's in there?" Sharon asked, as her brother rushed up breathlessly.

As Randy opened the bag, Sue exclaimed, "Bananas! Are they for us to eat?"

"Of course not," Randy said. "How can a detective find a monkey without bananas to lure him?"

"That's a good idea, Randy," Sharon said. "Come on! Let's look for monkey footprints."

The four walked slowly along until Sue cried out, "I see some!"

Tiny markings, pressed lightly into the sand, led to the water's edge, where several dozen sandpipers ran through the lacy foam of the retreating waves.

"You silly!" Randy said. "They're not monkeys."

Sue giggled and pointed to three sad-looking pelicans skimming along the top of the waves.

"Are they playing a game?" she asked.

"They're looking for fish," Sharon replied.

Just then one of the pelicans dived into the surf. Seconds later it reappeared with a small silvery fish wriggling in its bill. Then the fish vanished into the pelican's pouch!

"Poor little fishy!" Sue remarked sadly, as the monkey search continued.

The children walked back and forth across the broad beach, their eyes intent on the hard gray sand.

"I don't think a monkey would stay too near the water," Sharon reasoned. "Let's look over there, around that shack with the trees."

"We'd better be careful," Randy warned them. "That's where old Alec Ferguson lives. He doesn't like children."

"We won't go too near the house," Pam said. "Just close enough to look into those palm trees."

"I think this is far enough," Randy said in a worried voice. "I don't want that old shrimp fisherman to chase us."

The children stopped and looked up into the branches of the palm trees.

"Listen! What's that?" Pam asked.

"Just the wind rustling the palm fronds," Sharon answered.

"If Lady Rhesus was up there," Randy said, "she'd come down for the bag of bananas, wouldn't she?"

He held the brown sack high overhead. "Lady Rhesus, here's some lunch." But the monkey did not appear. "Oh, well," Randy said with a sigh, "let's go back."

Turning quickly, the boy tripped over a piece of driftwood half covered with sand. "Oops!" he cried

"Oops!" he cried.

and fell sidewise, landing on top of the bag of bananas.

Squash!

Randy picked himself up and sheepishly opened the bag. The bananas had split open and were a gooey mess.

"That's not a very attractive lunch for Lady," his sister declared.

"You're right, but what will I do with them now?"

Pam suggested that they bury the bananas in the sand, so as not to clutter the beach front.

Randy bent down and started to scoop a hole. Suddenly he stopped short and pointed. "Hey, look at this!"

Faintly imprinted in the sand nearby were two tiny footprints.

"Randy, you've made a discovery!" Pam cried out.

The children fell on their hands and knees to examine the tiny markings. Wind-blown sand had nearly obscured them from sight.

"We're on the trail!" Sharon cried excitedly. "Let's see if we can find some more footprints."

Still on hands and knees, Sharon, Pam and Sue searched carefully while Randy buried the sack of bananas. Then he, too, joined them.

Sharon made an extra discovery—another set of footprints.

Pam stood up and studied the distance between the two sets of prints. "The monkey was running fast," she said, "and was headed right toward that shack."

"You're a good detective," Sharon said. "Come on. Let's see where the tracks lead."

"We're too close to the shack," Randy said, his eyes darting from the front to the back door of the dilapidated building. But there was no sign of the gruff fisherman.

"I can't find any more footprints," Sharon declared.

"Neither can I," Pam said with a perplexed look.

"Where did Lady go?" said Sue.

"She couldn't just have vanished," Sharon declared.

Before the cousins could think any more about this, they heard a strange muffled voice from inside the house.

"Oo!" Sue cried out. "We'd better run!"

The little girl dashed off, and the others were forced to follow her. She raced toward the beach, and did not stop until she was a safe distance from the shack.

"Oh dear," Pam said. "I wish we could have followed that clue. It's such a good one."

"Let's go tell Pete," Sharon suggested. "Maybe if we all go back——"

"Here he comes now," said Randy, looking far down the sandy shore.

As Pete, followed by Ricky and Holly, drew closer,

Pam could hear her older brother shouting. "Look! See what we've found!" he called out.

"What is it?"

"A treasure," Holly said.

In his right hand Pete waved a piece of dull, silver-colored metal.

"I think it's a piece of the rocket!" he cried out excitedly.

CHAPTER 7

A MYSTERIOUS VOICE

THE "treasure" which Pete held in his hand was about the size of a dinner plate. It was grayish white in color and had jagged edges.

"How wonderful!" Pam said. "Where did you find it?"

Pete said the metal was buried under water in the sand, with only a small part of the edge showing. "It looked like a broken clamshell. I nearly swam right past it."

"This may be a great discovery!" Randy declared proudly. "Come on, let's take it to Dad right away."

"Wait!" said Sharon, putting her hand on Pete's arm. "We have news too."

She quickly told about the monkey footprints and the strange noise the children had heard coming from inside the fisherman's shack.

"You mean, it might have been the monkey making them? Yikes!" Ricky exclaimed.

Pete was undecided whether he should hasten off to telephone his uncle or to examine the footprints the others had found. Finally he said, "As long as we're here, show Holly and Rick and me the prints."

"Follow me," Pam directed, retracing her steps across the beach.

"See!" Sharon called out a minute later. "The little prints are right over here."

"I can't find them," Holly said after looking around.

"I can't either," declared Ricky, squatting down to examine the sand more closely.

Pam, too, dropped to her knees, and scanned the area. Crestfallen, she said, "They're gone."

"How could that have happened?" Randy asked, puzzled. "They were here just a few minutes ago!"

Pete frowned. He could not understand such a thing himself. He glanced about in all directions.

"Maybe Alec Ferguson saw you out here and wiped out the prints after you left," he said.

"You mean," Sharon asked, "like a bad person getting rid of the evidence?"

"Exactly," Pete replied. "Who else could have done it?"

"Marshmallow could have," Holly said. "He may have been spying on us."

"That's right," Pam admitted. "See this place? It looks as if someone scraped his foot back and forth across the sand."

While the older children were trying to solve the mystery, Sue wandered off in the direction of the shack. Unseen by the others, she tiptoed up to one of the low windows. Hiding behind the shrubs, she peeked inside, hoping to see Lady Rhesus.

Pam was the first to discover that the little girl

had wandered off. "Oh!"she gasped. "Look where Sue is!"

Just then her dark-haired sister left the shack and dashed frantically toward the others. She tripped and fell on a piece of driftwood, but picked herself up and raced breathlessly to the other children.

"Oh, it was spooky! I saw it! I saw it! Something was jumping around!"

"What was it?" Pete asked.

"It looked like a monkey's shadow."

Had Sue imagined it all? Or had the little monkey been hopping about inside the shack?

"I think we'd all better look," Pete suggested.

"But what about Alec Ferguson?" Randy glanced ahead worriedly. "I don't want to meet that mean man again!"

"We'll have to take that chance," Pete said. "This is too good a clue to drop now."

Pete posted the others as lookouts, far enough from the shack so they would be in no danger from the fisherman. Then, walking back toward the beach, he hid the precious piece of metal in a tall clump of grass.

Returning, he whispered to Pam, "I'm going to creep up and look in that window. Just yell if anyone opens the door or walks toward the shack."

"Okay. But hurry."

Pete moved slowly toward the shack. Then suddenly he sprinted to the low shrubs near it and ducked behind them. He lay quiet for a minute.

Hearing nothing, he lifted his head until his eyes came level with the window sill.

Pete's eyes swept the gloomy interior. The only things he could see were a cot, an old table, two dilapidated chairs, and a lamp with a broken shade. On the floor lay a small tattered rug and scattered newspapers. There were no people or animals in sight.

It must have been Sue's imagination, Pete thought, when suddenly he was startled by a loud voice.

"What? Scrub that bird!"

Pete ducked his head. His heart pounded. There must be a missile man inside the fisherman's shack. But where was he? Pete wondered about staying to hear more or running away. The boy's mind was made up by the next words. "Who's there?" the deep voice said.

Pete scrambled out of the bushes and ran fast toward Pam, at the same time signaling to the other lookouts to move back. When all the children were at a safer distance, Pam said breathlessly, "What did you see, Pete?"

"Nobody. But someone's in there. A missile man. I heard him talking."

"Maybe Alec Ferguson is sharing his place with a missile man from Cape Canaveral," Sharon suggested. "I heard Mother say it's hard for the men to find places to rent."

"I don't think a missile man would live in that old shack," Pete ventured.

Pete's eyes swept the gloomy interior.

"But what about Lady Rhesus?" Sue asked. "Did you see her?"

"No," Pete replied. "You must have imagined that you did."

The little girl felt hurt that nobody believed her story and bravely held back tears that welled into her eyes. "I just know that Lady is in there! The missile man is going to put her in the rocket and shoot her to the moon," Sue said. As Pam put a comforting arm about her sister, Pete walked over to the clump of grass where he had hidden the piece of metal from a rocket. It was not where he had placed it. Frantically the boy parted every blade of grass, but in vain.

"It's gone!" he cried out. "Somebody's taken it!"

Pete looked up and down the beach. In the distance he saw a boy running away.

"There's the one who took it!" he cried out.

"It looks like Marsh!" Randy declared.

"Don't let him get away!" Pam shouted, racing after the boy.

Spurred on by his desire to recover the important clue, Pete sprinted over the sand like a fleeing antelope. Soon he could plainly see that the boy ahead was indeed Marshall Holt.

"Stop! Give that back to me!" Pete shouted.

Marsh glanced over his shoulder for a second and ran faster. Suddenly he swerved from the beach and raced along a sandy lane.

Ahead Pete could see a bicycle propped against

a palm tree. Marsh flung himself onto the saddle. Pete was now only a few feet behind him.

"Stop, I tell you!" Pete cried, as Marsh started to pedal off.

In desperation Pete made a lunge at the back wheel. He missed by inches and sprawled in the lane!

CHAPTER 8

CONGRATULATIONS TO PETE

SCRAMBLING to his feet, Pete raced after Marshall Holt, who was pedaling furiously down the sandy lane. He was steering with one hand and holding the piece of metal in the other.

Suddenly the front wheel of Marsh's bicycle hit a rut filled with deep sand, and it stopped short, sending Marsh over the handlebars. He landed on his side with a thud.

"Now we can catch him!" Ricky cried gleefully, running beside Pete, with the other cousins at their heels.

They quickly surrounded the thrown rider, who rose slowly, clutching his right arm. Meanwhile, Pete bent down to pick up the metal, which lay beside the bicycle.

"Now we have you!" Randy cried out.

When Sharon noticed Marsh wincing with pain she asked, "Are you hurt?"

The boy nodded. "I landed on a sharp stone," he said.

Pam saw that Marsh's elbow was badly skinned and swollen. "Let me help you," she said kindly.

"He ought to get a punch," Ricky protested.

"Hush!" Pam told her brother. "If he's hurt, we should help him. She turned to Pete. "Have you a clean handkerchief?"

"Sure." He pulled a freshly pressed one from his pocket.

Pam took it and bandaged the injured elbow. Marsh seemed embarrassed by such kind treatment. "Thanks a lot," he said.

"But I still think you had an awful nerve to run off with this," Pete said, holding up the metal.

"I was only trying to help," Marsh replied sheepishly.

"Do you call spying on us helping?" Ricky demanded.

Marsh hung his head. He admitted that he had spied on the cousins and had observed Pam when she had discovered the monkey tracks.

"I thought I'd get even by wiping out the monkey footprints," he said.

"If you play any more mean tricks on us, you'll be sorry," Pete warned. "Holly nearly got hurt when she climbed the oak tree looking for Lady Rhesus."

"I'm sorry for that," Marsh said, and he sounded sincere. "I thought Pete would climb the tree instead of Holly."

"How did you expect to help us by running off with the piece of metal?" Sharon demanded.

Marsh explained that he wanted to be of assistance to the missile men. "I expect to be an astronaut myself someday," he said.

"Well, that's no way to do it," Pam said. She picked up the fallen bicycle, and Pete held it steady while Marsh mounted it.

"So long," he said, embarrassed, and rode away.

Pam gazed after him until he disappeared onto the main road. "I think Marsh really is sorry," she said.

"I'm not so sure," Pete commented dubiously. "He'll have to prove it to me."

The children hastened to the nearby motel, where Pete phoned his aunt. After he told her about the discovery, she said, "Good work, Pete. I'll call your Uncle Walt. I'm sure he'll come to pick you up right away and take the metal to the laboratory. But all of you can't fit into the Bug. Wait where you are and I'll drive right over."

Aunt Carol in the station wagon and Uncle Walt in the Bug arrived at the same time.

"What do you think of this?" Pete said, handing his uncle the chunk of metal. "Is it important?"

The missile man turned it over in his hands, studying the piece carefully. "Pete," he said, "this definitely is part of old Thuzzy. It may solve the mystery of why she blew up! We'll take it to the laboratory."

When all of the cousins clamored to go with him, Aunt Carol said, "The younger children will come with me." Holly, Sue, and Ricky obeyed without a word of protest.

Pete, Pam, Sharon, and Randy squeezed into the Bug with Uncle Walt. Waving good-by to the others, they headed south along the highway toward Patrick Air Force Base.

The road skirted the ocean, which rolled and pounded to their left. On the right were clusters of small houses, behind which they could glimpse the calm water of the Banana River. Ten minutes later the sprawling buildings of the base came into view.

"Crickets," Pete said, "I didn't know it was this large!"

Low barracks and taller buildings occupied a wide area, past which the hangars of a great airport loomed in the distance.

"It's a regular town," Randy commented, as his father drove through one of the gates and into the grounds of the military post. He pulled up in front of a long white building and parked at the curb.

"Stay here until I return," he said. "I shan't be long."

"Okay, Dad," Randy said, sliding into the driver's seat.

As soon as the missile man had disappeared into the laboratory building, his son turned to Pete, seated beside him.

"Let's play a game of auto racing," he said.

"Sure, Randy. You be the driver and I'll be your mechanic."

Beaming delightedly, Randy grasped the steering wheel. "Hang on tight, everybody, and imagine we're at Daytona Beach, where the auto races are held."

Pam and Sharon exchanged winks and told Randy

he could go as fast as he liked, just so long as he did not bump into any other cars.

"*Rumpf, rumpf, rumpf,*" Randy said, making a noise like a racing car shifting gears. At the same time he swayed back and forth, turning the wheel first to the left, then to the right.

"Gangway! I'm threading my way through the pack!" he cried out.

Randy was having such a good time that the others laughed. "Step on the gas!" Pete called out; and, "Pass that fellow in front of us."

"He won't get out of the way," Randy said. "I'll just blow my horn." Randy pressed his hand on the horn. It blared, startling several passers-by, but when the youngster removed his hand, the horn still kept on blowing.

Randy looked startled. "It won't stop!" he cried.

Pete leaned over and jiggled the horn, but still it kept sounding. Now several faces appeared at the windows of the laboratory and people stopped on the street to stare at the Bug.

Just then a group of men walked up. Pete noticed that each wore a round plastic tag on his lapel bearing the word "Press," and he guessed that they were newspaper reporters.

One of the men hastened to the car and said to Pete, "Having trouble?"

"We can't stop the horn."

"I'll help you," the man offered. "Release the hood lock."

"The horn won't stop blowing!" he cried.

Randy did this. The man lifted the hood and disconnected some wires. The horn stopped blowing.

"Thank you," Pete said, as the man closed the hood.

"Glad to help you," he replied smiling. "My name is Willard of the Chicago *Globe*."

"We're the Hollisters," Pete said, nodding toward his sister, "and these are our cousins, Sharon and Randy Davis."

"My dad's a missile man," Randy said proudly.

"In that case, he'll be able to repair the horn," Mr. Willard said. "So long, children."

As he hurried off to rejoin the other reporters, Sharon said, "Do you know what, Pam? I think these reporters are here for a special reason."

"What do you mean?"

Sharon leaned close to Pam's ear and whispered, "I think there's going to be a big rocket shoot, and those men are here to report it for their newspapers."

Before her cousin had a chance to comment, Uncle Walt strode out of the lab building and walked to the car. "Was that our horn I heard?" he asked.

"Yes, Dad," Randy said sheepishly. "I think I broke it."

"Nothing of the sort," his father replied, chuckling. "That happened once before."

When Pete told how Mr. Willard had loosened the wires, Uncle Walt lifted the hood and tinkered with the horn for a few seconds.

"Try it now, Randy," he said.

The boy beeped the horn.

"There—now it's okay," his father said, and took his place at the wheel of the Bug.

"Uncle Walt," Pete said as the motor started, "what did they think about the piece of metal?"

His uncle smiled. "You're to be congratulated, Pete." He said that the technicians thought Pete had found an excellent clue. "We may even learn from it why old Thuzzy blew up!"

"That's swell," said Randy.

As the Bug drove out of the Air Force base and onto the main highway, Pam leaned over the front seat. "Uncle Walt," she said quietly, "is another bird going to fly the coop tonight?"

At first the question startled the missile man, but he soon laughed. "Who told you—— I mean, what makes you think so, Pam?"

"All those newspapermen. Sharon thought of it."

Uncle Walt merely smiled and remained silent for several seconds. Then he replied, "I can't tell any official secrets, but how would you children like to have a beach party tonight?"

CHAPTER 9

A TRICK

SHARON hugged her father and said, "Oh, thanks, Daddy! Beach parties are such fun!"

"Mother knows about it already," Uncle Walt informed his daughter.

Sharon told her cousins that beach parties at Cape Canaveral were shared by hundreds of people. Whenever word of a night shoot leaked out, families of the missile men would gather on the shore line to watch the fiery display in the evening sky.

"Will another Thuzzy go up this evening?" Pete asked excitedly.

"Maybe."

When the four cousins arrived home, the rest of the family were busy preparing for the cookout. The kitchen table was laden with hamburger meat, rolls, relish, and fruit, which Aunt Carol packed into a picnic hamper. Holly helped her mother put bottles of soda into a cooler, while Ricky folded a large beach blanket and carried it to the station wagon.

"Oh, we've had such an exciting day," Pam said, and went over the events step by step.

"Mr. Ferguson's shack certainly sounds mysterious," Aunt Carol said, as she packed a jar of pickles into the hamper. "How do you suppose we can find out if Lady Rhesus is in it?"

"Why don't you try a direct approach?" Uncle Walt suggested.

"What do you mean, Walter?" his wife asked.

"Go right up, knock on the door, and ask the man if he has found the monkey. He may be perfectly innocent."

"A grown-up could do that, Dad," Randy said, "but not children. Alec Ferguson doesn't like them."

"Suppose you knock on the door, Daddy?" Sharon said.

"Sorry, children, but I won't be with you on the picnic tonight," Uncle Walt said, grinning boyishly.

"Then there *will* be a missile shoot!" Randy exclaimed.

His father did not reply. Instead Aunt Carol winked at the children. "Our daddy is so mysterious about the missiles."

"They are my babies and I have to take care of them," the missile man replied.

He said good-by, wished them all a gay time at the beach party, and set off for Cape Canaveral in the Bug.

Ricky looked disappointed to see his uncle leave, but realized that work on the Cape was more important than a picnic. He turned to his mother and said, "Now who's going to knock on Alec Ferguson's door?"

"I'll volunteer," Mrs. Hollister said.

"Goody! Mother's not afraid!" Sue exclaimed. "If there is a monkey inside, she'll find out."

Soon the picnickers were ready. After the boys had carried the hamper and jugs to the back of the station wagon, Sharon called out, "Missy, Missy, come on, we're going to the beach!"

A little brown nose was poked out of the bushes and the little dachshund scampered to her mistress.

"You shouldn't be home alone when a missile is going to be shot. You'll tell us even before we hear it."

Traffic to the beach was heavy. A long line of cars threaded over the causeway toward the Atlantic shore.

Nearing the beach, Pam glanced at Cape Canaveral. Rays of the late afternoon sun glinted off tall metal towers which looked like great oil derricks in the distance.

"Those are the gantries," Randy said, "the rocket work platforms."

"Daddy says the proper name for the gantry is service tower," Sharon added.

"But how tiny they are!" Holly said.

"They only look that way because they are miles from here," Aunt Carol explained. "They're really very tall." She told the Hollisters that the missiles stood about one hundred feet high on the launching pads.

"Yikes!" Ricky exclaimed. "I'd like to see them close up sometime."

Aunt Carol said she was sorry, but this might not

be possible. Children were not allowed on the missile range except in very unusual cases. One of those times was when the children of the Dutch queen got a close-up look. "And also the grandchildren of the President of the United States," she added.

By the time the Hollisters and their cousins reached the waterfront, cars were streaming onto the beach. Sharon directed her mother to a spot near Alec Ferguson's shack. Aunt Carol parked the car so it headed toward the water. The children climbed out.

"Here's a dandy place for a fire," Pete said, running over to a small depression in the sand.

Ricky and Randy raced about looking for driftwood and soon returned with their arms full. Meanwhile, Pam had spread the blanket and Pete had unloaded the food and drinks from the back of the car.

Missy seemed to be as excited as the children. She wagged her tail and ran around in circles, kicking up little sprays of sand.

Excitement ran like chain lightning all along the beach front, where other families were preparing their suppers.

"Tonight's shoot must be very important," Sharon suggested. "Maybe they'll send Thuzzy into outer space."

As evening shadows crept over the beach, one bonfire after another sprang to life, giving the shore a festive appearance.

"Maybe we should call on Alec Ferguson before it gets too late," Mrs. Hollister suggested.

"That's a good idea," Aunt Carol agreed. "Randy, suppose you and Ricky guard the fire, while the rest of us ask the fisherman about the monkey."

"Yes, Mother."

The other children, led by their mothers, marched across the dunes toward the shack. Without hesitation Mrs. Hollister knocked on the door. It opened a crack, and through it Pete could see the face of the shrimp fisherman. "What do you want?" the man asked gruffly.

"I'm Mrs. Hollister. A friend of ours lost a pet monkey. Because of its footprints in the sand, we thought she might be in your house."

Before Alec Ferguson had a chance to reply, another voice from inside the shack called, "What do they want?"

The fisherman closed the door a moment, then opened it again. "We don't have any monkey here," he said, and slammed the door.

"What a rude man!" Pam declared, as they turned back toward the picnic spot.

"At least we know he doesn't have Lady Rhesus," Mrs. Hollister said, "but he could have answered more politely."

Walking across the sand, Pete whispered to Pam, "I don't think Alec Ferguson's telling the truth. . . . Oh, look! Here comes Mr. Jeep."

The friendly man was driving slowly past the gay

knots of picnickers. When he saw the Hollisters and the Davises he stopped and waved to them.

"Hi, Mr. Jeep!" Pete called out. "I'd like to introduce you to my mother and Aunt Carol."

"How do you do," the man said, and added with a wink at the children, "How are the young detectives making out?"

"We're baffled," Pam spoke up. "Perhaps you can help us."

"Glad to, if I can."

"Does Alec Ferguson live alone?"

"As far as I know, he does."

"Well," Pete said, "there's somebody else in that shack with him."

"It could be a friend," Mr. Jeep added with a shrug. "Well, I have to get along. Business should be good tonight. Have a good time, and I hope you find the monkey."

Ricky and Randy had a brisk fire burning by the time the others returned and Missy was sniffing at the bag containing the hamburgers.

"You'll have to wait, Missy," Sharon said. "We'll feed you later."

The dachshund barked sharply, then scampered off.

"Won't she get lost?" Pam asked worriedly.

"Not Missy," Sharon laughed. "She loves to romp on the beach. She'll be back."

Aunt Carol gave each of the children individual grills with long wire handles. Then Mrs. Hollister inserted plump hamburgers into each grill and the cousins held them over the embers. Soon the tempting aroma of sizzling meat mingled with the fresh sea air. The lapping waves and crackling fire added to the enjoyment of the beach picnic.

"This is good fun!" Pam said, as she slipped her hamburger between the halves of a soft bun.

"Relish, catchup, or mustard, Ricky?" Aunt Carol asked.

"All, thank you!" he replied, helping himself to generous portions of each.

Sharon meanwhile poured cool frothy soda into tall paper cups and handed them out to the others. As they ate, it grew darker. The beach fires gleamed more brightly along the broad stretch of gray sand.

"And now for a little surprise," Aunt Carol said. "Ice cream and cake for dessert."

She opened an insulated paper bag containing a gallon of ice cream, and began scooping it onto paper plates. Just as the picnickers were finishing the delicious dessert, Missy trotted up to the bonfire. In her mouth she held a small package.

"Goodness, what's that?" Aunt Carol asked.

"Oh, dear!" Pam replied. "It's a package of frankfurters."

"Missy, you naughty girl," Sharon said. "Where did you get them?"

The dachshund backed away, shaking her head.

"Drop it!" Randy ordered, scrambling toward the

"Missy, you naughty dog!" Sharon said.

pet. Missy did not obey. Instead she ran around in circles.

Finally Sharon offered the dog a bit of hamburger. Missy dropped the package of frankfurters and gobbled the tidbit.

Randy picked up the package. Fortunately the dog's teeth had not punctured the transparent wrapper.

Mrs. Hollister sighed. "Some family's going to miss a meal if we don't find out who owns the frankfurters."

"I'll try to locate the owner," Pam volunteered, rising from the blanket.

"And I'll go with her," Pete said.

The two children took the package and walked along the beach in the direction from which Missy had come. As they passed each group of picnickers they asked whether or not anyone had lost the frankfurters. One after the other, the answer was "No."

Next, three people came into view, sitting around a flickering fire. As Pam approached them, she gave a little gasp. "Oh, look, Pete! There's Marshall Holt."

"That must be his mother and father," Pete whispered.

As the Hollisters approached the fire Pete said, "Hello, Marsh. The Davises' dog ran off with these franks. Are they yours?"

"Yes, they are," the boy replied. "Thanks," he said, taking the package.

Slightly embarrassed, Marsh introduced Pete and

Pam to his mother and father. They were a pleasant-looking couple.

"I'm glad to meet you," Mr. Holt said. He paused a moment before going on, "I hope that you and Marshall will become friends."

Pete grinned. "I guess we didn't have such a good start, did we, Marsh?"

"I'm sorry for the mean tricks I played on you," the older boy said.

Marsh quickly broke open the package of frankfurters, speared three of them on a long metal skewer, and held them over the fire.

"Marshall tells us that you are a family of detectives," his mother said, smiling.

Pete and Pam admitted they had solved several mysteries and Pam added, "It's fun doing things for other people."

"I'd like to help you solve mysteries," Marsh said. "May I?"

"Of course," Pete replied. "Well, we must go back. See you later." Brother and sister trotted off across the sand.

"Marsh is changing, isn't he?" Pam remarked.

"He's not such a bad guy after all," Pete said. "Maybe we've found a new friend in him."

"Pete," said Pam worriedly, "I can't get Lady Rhesus out of my mind. If she's in Mr. Ferguson's shack, she'll be safe when the missile blasts off. But the monkey may have gone to the Cape and be hiding near the launching pad. Right now she may be in great danger."

"Crickets! I hope you're wrong!" her brother replied.

Back at their own campfire Pam said, "You'll never guess who owned the frankfurters," and told how friendly Marsh and his family had been.

Just then Missy, who was lying quietly in Sharon's arms, began to shake and whine.

"Missile! Missile!" the children shouted in loud voices. Immediately the cries went up along the beach and the sky lighted up over Cape Canaveral.

"There goes Thuzzy!" Randy cried out, jumping up and down with excitement.

"It looks like a million Fourths of July," Ricky declared.

The rocket rose slowly into the night sky, amidst a great puff of white smoke and orange flames.

Everybody on the beach stood up and cheered, as the rocket streaked higher and higher. But Pam's thoughts still dwelled on Lady Rhesus. Even before the missile was out of sight, the girl turned wistfully toward the fisherman's shack. Lights glowed at the windows. Was Lady still inside, a prisoner of Alec Ferguson?

The night air still was filled with shouts and clapping of the missile onlookers when Pam was startled to see a crack of light at the door of the shack. It opened a few inches. Then something small and dark slipped out and the door closed.

Pam's pulse raced. "Oh, it just can't be true!" she told herself, hardly daring to hope for such good fortune. "But if that *was* Lady Rhesus . . ."

She raced away from the other picnickers without being noticed as the rocket winked out of sight in the black velvet sky. "Lady! Lady! Come to Pam!" the girl cried out as she stumbled through the darkened fringe of beach, lightened here and there by the fitful glow of the bonfires, calling again and again.

Finally, not ten feet from her, the tiny figure of a monkey glided out of the shadows and slowly approached Pam.

"Lady, it's you!" Pam bent down gently, so as not to frighten the little animal. "Please come here," she begged.

Lady Rhesus hesitated and took a step backward. Could Pam capture her or not?

CHAPTER 10

FORBIDDEN TERRITORY

LADY Rhesus seemed undecided about whether she wished to be caught by Pam or continue her freedom as a runaway. The little animal sat still, blinking her eyes and scratching herself.

Pam continued to coax the small animal. "Please come to me," she begged, bending down and holding her arms wide open.

Lady Rhesus took a few steps forward. Then with a leap she landed on the girl's shoulder. Pam hurried back to her group.

"The monkey!" they exclaimed.

Sue cheered and clapped. "Lady didn't go up in the sky after all!"

Pam told how she had captured Lady Rhesus. "Alec Ferguson *did* have her!"

"Yes," Mrs. Hollister agreed. "I'm glad he let her go, so that mystery is solved."

"Why did you run away?" Sharon scolded Lady Rhesus.

The monkey chattered, blinked, and hopped to Pam's other shoulder. It was then that the girl noticed something black clutched in the animal's paw.

"What are you holding?" Pam asked her.

As if understanding every word the girl had said, Lady Rhesus opened her fingers. A black feather fell to the ground.

Pam bent down to pick it up. "A crow's feather, I guess," she said, and showed it to Pete.

"I haven't seen any crows around here," he remarked, perplexed.

"Maybe Alec Ferguson had a stuffed crow and the monkey played with it," Ricky suggested.

"If the feather was green or red or blue," Pam said, "I'd think it came from a talking parrot in the shack."

"That's right," Pete agreed. "Sailors and fishermen often keep parrots as pets, but I've never heard of a black parrot."

"If Alec caught the monkey," Randy wondered, "why did he free her just at this time?"

"He knew we suspected him and he would have had to get in touch with the police to find the owner," Pam answered. "And for some reason perhaps he doesn't want to meet them."

"Alec's a suspicious character, all right," Aunt Carol declared. "Well," she added, as she tossed the paper picnic plates into the fire, "we've had plenty of excitement for one evening. Let's take Lady Rhesus to Miss Mott and then go home."

When the rubbish had been burned, and sand scattered on the bonfire, the cousins packed everything into the station wagon and Aunt Carol drove off.

"Maybe the monkey's mother has gone to bed already," said Sue with a big yawn.

The others laughed and Pam said, "You mean Miss Mott. But good news like this can't wait."

Aunt Carol and Mrs. Hollister agreed, so they drove directly to the Mott cottage on the Banana River. Lights burned in the house.

When the car pulled up in front, Sue was asleep in Pam's arms. Pete gently placed her in the back seat while the other children tiptoed to the front door of the cottage. The monkey began to chatter and jump around. She made so much noise that the lady artist heard her pet and came running to the door.

"Lady Rhesus!" she exclaimed. "Thank goodness you're safe!" The monkey jumped to her shoulder. To the children she said, "This is wonderful. Where did you find my little scamp?"

After Pam had related their experience, Miss Mott hurried to the kitchen and returned with a banana. Lady peeled the fruit and munched it contentedly.

"What can I ever do to repay you nice people?" Miss Mott said, stroking her pet. Then her eyes twinkled. "I know! How would you all like to take a ride in my boat tomorrow?"

"Oh, thank you so much," Pam said. "We girls have to go shopping for Florida playclothes."

Pete, however, accepted the offer, saying he would like to explore the river in a search for the missing nose cone of the exploded missile.

"Yipes!" Ricky exclaimed. "And we could fish at the same time."

"I'm all for it," Randy said happily.

"My boat will be ready for you in the morning," Miss Mott promised.

The children thanked her, said good night, and went to the car. When they arrived at the Davis home, Pete carried Sue inside. She awakened, rubbed her eyes sleepily, and walked into her bedroom to undress.

Just then Uncle Walt appeared in his pajamas and robe. "How did you like the show?" he asked with a grin.

"It was great!" Pete declared.

"A dilly!" Ricky said.

"Did the bird fly down range?" Randy asked his father.

Uncle Walt looked at the ceiling and pointed up. "No," he said. "Old Thuzzy is now in outer space."

"Oh, that's marvelous. I'll bet you're happy," Pam said.

"Indeed I am."

Uncle Walt said the cameras in the nose cone were sending back pictures already. "Our greatest feat so far," he added. "I'm glad the Hollisters were here to see it."

The missile man was pleased to hear that the monkey had been found and that the boys planned to search for the lost nose cone in the Banana River.

"The Air Force thinks that the pay load fell into the

Atlantic Ocean," Uncle Walt said, "but you never can tell about a freak explosion. Part of the missile may have landed in the Banana River."

"Then we'd better take our diving masks as well as fishing poles," Pete suggested.

"Good idea," Uncle Walt said. He also agreed with the others that Alec Ferguson was a suspicious character and added, "Perhaps I can get the security police to check on him."

The quiet living room suddenly was filled with a shriek from Sue. The little girl, clad in pajamas, dashed from her bedroom. "A spider!" she cried. "A giant spider is after me."

"I'll kill it," Ricky volunteered and dashed toward the bedroom.

"Wait! Stop!" Sharon called. "Don't kill the spider. It's an old friend of ours."

Ricky turned abruptly, an incredulous look on his face. "A friend?" he asked.

"Yes," Sharon went on. "Was the spider in the closet, Sue?"

"Yes," the little girl quavered.

Sharon explained that this was a "housekeeper" spider, so called because it kept other bugs and insects out of the house. "It won't hurt human beings," she said.

The Hollister cousins were eager to see the housekeeper spider and tiptoed into the bedroom. The friendly spider had a small black body and long thin legs. Hearing them, it scooted off behind some shoes.

"Oh, I'm so sorry to frighten you, Mrs. House-keeper," Sue declared with another yawn. With that she climbed into her bed and was sound asleep in moments.

The three boys arose early next morning, ate break-fast before the girls did, and climbed into the Bug. Uncle Walt, meanwhile, had gone to his sports locker in the utility room and pulled out three fishing poles.

"All right, fellows," he said, passing the poles through the window of the car. "Catch something really big today—such as the nose cone that the Air Force is still looking for!"

"We'll try," Pete assured his uncle with a grin.

In a few minutes, the missile man had left the boys in front of Miss Mott's house and driven off. The artist, who was waiting, showed them how to operate her motorboat, which bobbed in the water alongside her dock.

"The trout are biting well, I understand," she said, as Pete stepped in to man the tiller.

"We're after a bigger prize," Randy said, winking at his cousin.

"I hope you catch it," Miss Mott remarked.

As soon as he and Ricky had taken their seats, Miss Mott untied the line and pushed the craft out. Pete started the outboard motor. Then, waving good-by, the three boys headed down the Banana River.

Randy explained that Merritt Island lay to their right, while Cape Canaveral was on the left. As the sun rose higher, the boys could make out the launching site's service towers, which they had seen from the beach the evening before.

As the cousins cruised along, paying out their fishing lines, they kept looking into the water for any sign of the missing nose cone.

Suddenly Randy shouted, "Oh, oh, I've got something!" His pole bent as he reeled in a plump trout.

In a few minutes Ricky caught one, then Pete.

"Yikes!" Ricky declared. "This is great fun. We'll have a good mess of fish for dinner tonight."

"But I'd rather have a cone," Pete said chuckling. "And not the eating kind, either. Come on, fellows! Let's pay more attention to our search."

"Okay," Randy chimed in. "We can always catch fish."

As Ricky slowly reeled in his line he scanned the rippling waters of the river. In the distance, near the Canaveral shore, he saw a slender rod sticking up above the surface. Instantly he envisioned a round satellite lying on the bottom of the river with part of its antenna showing.

"Look! There it is!" Ricky called. "The pay load!"

"Crickets! It might be," Pete said, steering in that direction.

All at once Ricky's line was nearly wrenched from his hand. "Wow!" he cried. "I must have a whale on the end of this!"

He tried to reel in, but whatever was on the end of his line kept pulling harder than ever. Suddenly a

"Look!" Ricky called. "The sunken payload!"

large, dark object appeared on the surface of the water fifty feet from the boat.

Pete gasped. "It's a giant turtle!" he exclaimed.

"What'll I do?" Ricky called out desperately, hanging onto his pole.

"Don't let him get away!" Randy cried. "You've caught a grandfather turtle!"

"The turtle's caught me!" Ricky cried in dismay. "Help!"

Pete rose from his seat and grabbed the pole. Together the two boys tried to hoist the turtle toward their boat. But the giant shellback had no intention of being made into turtle soup. He swam one way, then reversed and swam the other. Suddenly the turtle jerked the line, and Ricky, standing close to the gunwale, was yanked overboard.

"Help! Help! The turtle's going to get me!" he yelled in alarm.

"He's gone!" Randy shouted. "Look! The line's broken."

Ricky splashed about and reached for the side of the boat, thrashing wildly as if a hundred giant turtles were after him.

With one strong pull Pete hauled Ricky aboard. The dripping-wet boy asked, "Is that antenna still out there in the water, Pete?"

"It is. I'm heading for it."

"Oh, I hope it's the lost nose cone!" Randy said in a whisper. "Dad'll be so proud of us if we find it."

Ricky meanwhile had shed his shirt and sneakers

and donned his diving mask and flippers. "I'm all wet anyhow," he said. "Let me dive under and take a look. Oh boy! I hope—I hope!"

As they neared the protruding rod, Ricky took a deep breath and dived over the side of the boat. Pete and Randy tingled with excitement as they watched the younger boy disappear beneath the surface. Would he find the missing nose cone? And if he did, how would they raise it from the river bottom?

The seconds that passed seemed like minutes to the eager watchers. Then they saw Ricky's head bob up like a cork alongside the rod. He whipped the mask from his face and frowned.

"It's only an old TV antenna stuck in the mud," he said, and climbed back into the boat.

Pete and Randy sighed in disappointment. "Maybe it was blown off a cottage in a storm."

In the excitement, the three boys had not noticed dark clouds gathering in the west. Now the wind freshened and the low clouds blotted out the sun as they blew toward Cape Canaveral.

"It looks like we're in for a windstorm," Randy warned the others. "They're bad around here. Come on, Pete, we'd better start the motor and head home."

Pete pressed the starter but the motor would not respond. Again and again he tried, but with no success. The wind, meanwhile, had kicked up little whitecaps on the Banana River, sending the boat toward the Canaveral shore.

"Let's not get too close to that place over there,"

Randy said, pointing. "Nobody but the missile men are allowed on Cape Canaveral."

"What are we going to do?" Pete asked, as the boat gathered speed toward the sandy beach.

Randy suggested that they try to row. In the bottom of the boat lay two oars, which Randy and Pete fitted into the locks, and each took an oar. But row as they might, the boys could not overcome the force of the wind and the waves.

Pete stood up and peered through the overcast weather toward the Cape, looming up toward them. "There's a big rocket on the pad nearest us!" he exclaimed.

The others turned to gaze at the white missile, which was poised alongside the service tower. From near the top issued a small stream of white smoke.

"Look at the LOX," Randy said. "They're getting that missile ready for firing."

"What's LOX?" Ricky asked, as the boys strained at the oars.

Randy explained that LOX stood for liquid oxygen. Some of it vaporizes as it is pumped into the missile.

As the boat was swept closer to the shore, the younger boys became very alarmed. Pete tried to appear calm.

But it was a losing battle. Five minutes later the keel scraped on the sandy bottom. They were stuck!

"Crickets!" Pete cried out. "We're on Cape Canaveral! This is forbidden territory!"

CHAPTER 11

AN UNDERGROUND ROCKET

"If it's forbidden territory," Ricky said, "let's shove off!"

"We'd only keep drifting back," Pete explained. "We'll have to go for help."

"Okay, if you say so."

Ricky kicked off his shoes, removed his socks, rolled up his trousers, and stepped out into the shallow water on the shore of Cape Canaveral.

As Pete and Randy moved to the back of the boat, Ricky pulled the craft up onto the sand. Pete and Randy hopped out, and all three boys pulled the boat to a spot so it would not float away.

"Now what'll we do?" Randy asked, as he gazed across the Cape toward the towering gantries.

"People here may think we're spies," Ricky declared. "The FBI will get after us!"

Pete had to smile at this. "Just a couple of midget spies," he said, teasing the younger boys. "I don't think they'll arrest us, but they might chase us off pronto."

The wind had died down, and rifts appeared in the low-hanging clouds, letting the sun shine through.

Over the tops of the tall marsh grass, Pete saw

several cars moving along a road not far from them.

"That ought to lead us to some help," Pete said, and pushed on toward the highway.

Just then the rackety noise of a helicopter sounded overhead, and the boys looked up to see a single rotor aircraft hovering above them.

"Oh-oh!" Ricky said. "They've spotted us!"

"It's a search plane looking for prowlers," Randy said worriedly.

From the moment the boys had set foot on the shore, Pete had wondered about security measures. The Cape, he thought, would be surrounded either by a high wire fence or by a line of soldiers patrolling the place. Since the area had neither, Pete agreed that the helicopter was indeed searching for spies.

Ricky and Randy flattened themselves against the tall grass. But Pete stood up and waved. The pilot apparently did not see them, for the craft moved away rapidly.

Pete bent down to pull Ricky and Randy to their feet. "Stand up and let's get going; otherwise people really will think you're a couple of spies."

"If I could only find dad," Randy said unhappily as they trudged toward the road, "he could help us out of this mess."

The farther the boys walked, the more gantries they saw.

"Golly," said Randy, "this is just like the pictures."

"What pictures?" Ricky asked.

Randy said that his father had shown him aerial pictures of Cape Canaveral. "Those gantries over there," he said, pointing toward the northeast, "are where the first Titan missile was launched. And over there were the Atlas complexes."

"What's a complex?" Pete asked as they trudged on.

Randy felt important that he knew the facts about the missile range. He explained that the complex meant the entire launching area of a single missile. "That includes the gantry and the blockhouse and launch support equipment."

Pete chuckled. "It does sound complex, all right, but I don't see any blockhouse."

As they walked on, Randy explained that a blockhouse was not a house, nor was it shaped like a block. "See those low mounds?" he asked.

"The things that look like igloos?" Ricky asked.

"Yes. Those are the blockhouses. Inside are all the instruments. Dad says they have television cameras showing everything that's happening on the launching pads."

Pete recalled reading about these blockhouses. They had thick roofs of concrete and sand to protect the missile men from the intense heat when the rockets blasted off.

"Well, here's the road," Pete said, leading the boys out of the tall grass. "I hope a car comes along soon." But none appeared.

About a quarter of a mile down the road loomed

a high wooden platform which seemed to be built atop dozens of telephone poles. A stairway led to the top of it, and several people were climbing up.

"Let's go over there and get help," Pete suggested.

The cousins ran along the road. Several cars were parked at the foot of the platform, but they were empty. From the top, voices drafted down.

Ricky led the way up the steep steps. When they were halfway to the top, a deep voice sounded as if from a loudspeaker, "Minus ten and holding!"

"Crickets!" Pete cried out. "There's going to be a shoot!"

When the boys reached the top they saw a group of men and women. Some were jotting down notes while others scanned the Cape with field glasses.

Suddenly Randy cried out, "Pete, look! There's Mr. Willard."

"Say, everyone is wearing those round tags," Pete said. "This must be a reporter's observation platform."

"Hello, Mr. Willard!" Randy called, running toward the friendly man.

The reporter looked at the three boys in disbelief. "How did you get up here?"

"It's all a mistake," Ricky said. "We're not spies —really we're not." And he told about their stranded boat on the Banana River.

"So you were searching for the nose cone and hooked a turtle instead." The reporter laughed. "Now, who would believe that story?"

"It's true!" Ricky protested. "Isn't it, Randy?"

Mr. Willard clapped Ricky on the back. "Of course I believe you, and I think you boys are mighty patriotic, trying to locate the missing pay load."

The newspaperman quickly told the cousins that there were two guesses about what had happened at the time of the explosion. "Some officials," he said, "think that the nose cone was blown to bits, while others believe that it fell far out at sea."

"Then perhaps we'd better get a bigger boat and search offshore," Ricky said.

"But how can we do that without expensive diving equipment?" Randy asked.

Before Ricky could think up an answer to this, Mr. Willard interrupted, "Here's the man you boys are looking for!" He led them to a uniformed guard standing near the railing.

"Kelly," he said with a grin, "these three Martians parachuted down onto the Cape. They are posing as boys. What are we going to do with them?"

"I guess we could send them up in the rocket," Mr. Kelly said.

"Oh, I'd like a ride in Thuzzy," Ricky retorted.

"Thuzzy?" Mr. Kelly said. "Why, that's Walt Davis's pet name for the missile."

"He's my dad!" Randy said, stepping forward proudly, and then told about their boat's engine dying while they were looking for the nose cone.

A loudspeaker attached to the wooden railing

squealed and squawked. Then the deep voice said, "Resume countdown."

Mr. Willard and the guard moved off to one side and held a whispered consultation.

"Oh, I guess it's all right to let them stay here and watch the firing," Mr. Kelly said. "Come on, boys. Make yourselves at home with the rest of these newspaper, radio, and television people."

"Thank you," Pete said, relieved and happy.

"Here, use my glasses," the security man said, removing them from around his neck.

Pete trained the glasses on the tall missile from which the LOX was steaming.

"That's not the one," Mr. Kelly said.

Pete looked astounded. "Where is it then, Mr. Kelly?"

The security man explained that the scientists were about to shoot an underground rocket. "We're testing an advanced missile to be used in submarines. The first ones were called Polaris. Now look over there," he said, pointing.

Pete trained the binoculars on what looked like a small building. "Crickets! The roof is moving," Pete said. He gave Ricky and Randy each a turn using the glasses.

Mr. Willard explained that there was a huge hole in the ground, five stories deep. Inside the hole was a giant machine which could simulate the action of a ship in the water. "It pitches, rolls, and yaws," the reporter said. "The missile is fired from inside this contraption."

"But won't it burn up everything?" Pete asked.

"No, Pete. Do you know how an air gun works?" Mr. Willard said.

"Oh yes," Pete replied. "The air is pumped into a small space. When it's released, it shoots the pellet out."

"Exactly," the man continued. "And that is just how the submarine missile is launched."

He told the boys that a giant air gun was contained in the base of the device. It hurled the rocket high into the air, where it automatically ignited and went on its way.

"Minus ten seconds—nine—eight—seven—six," the squawk box blared.

The onlookers were tense with excitement. Would the new missile work or would it blow up?

Two of the reporters who had witnessed launchings many times before passed their binoculars to Ricky and Randy. The boys fixed their gaze on the underground launching pad.

"Five—four—three—two—one. Zero!"

Suddenly a long white missile leaped into the air. When it was high above the building, a burst of flame shot from its tail and with a rumbling roar it hurtled skyward. Nobody moved. No one said a word. All anxiously eyed the pencil-like rocket as it thundered down the Atlantic Missile Range. Not until it was out of sight did anyone speak.

"Great shot!" Mr. Willard said.

"Great shot!" Mr. Willard said.

"That was keen!" said Ricky, handing back the binoculars.

"Well, now that you have seen it, boys," Mr. Kelly said, "I'll take you back to your boat."

"But it won't start," Ricky said.

"I have an idea," the guard went on, "that you are out of fuel."

Pete's chin dropped. "I never thought of that," he said.

After thanking Mr. Willard, the three boys set off with the security guard. They went in his car to a nearby hangar, where Mr. Kelly obtained a five-gallon can of gasoline.

As they drove along the road, Pete asked about security regulations on the Cape.

The guard said that the launching complexes were guarded by tall metal fences but that it would be impossible to patrol the entire shore. He added, "We have had a little trouble recently with prowlers and picked up several."

"Were any named Ferguson?" Pete asked.

"No. Why?"

Pete told the guard about the shrimp fisherman and described Alec Ferguson.

"Well, if I should run into him I'll ask a few questions myself," Mr. Kelly said. "Here we are, boys. Let's park and walk over to your boat."

When they reached the craft, he stepped aboard

and opened the fuel tank. He grinned. "Dry, as I expected."

A sheepish look came over Pete's face as he helped Mr. Kelly fill the tank. "Thank you," he said. "I'd like to pay you for the gas."

"Glad to give it to you. Okay, boys, hop in and I'll shove you off. And better luck in your search for the pay load!"

In a few moments the motor was running again. As Pete, Ricky, and Randy waved good-by to the friendly guard, the craft moved through the calm waters in the direction of Miss Mott's bungalow.

They docked the boat, thanked Miss Mott, and telephoned to Randy's mother. She called for them soon afterward. Arriving home, the boys stormed through the front door, eager to tell their venture to everybody.

They were surprised to see Mr. Davis in the living room. At once Pete said, "Another failure, Uncle Walt. We didn't find the nose cone."

His uncle smiled. "Never mind. That piece of metal you did find a few days ago has solved a big mystery!"

CHAPTER 12

SNAP THE WHIP

"You mean it?" Pete cried jubilantly. "What kind of mystery?"

"The stress and strain in that piece of metal," Uncle Walt said, "showed why the missile exploded. The lab made the report this afternoon."

"Crickets, that's great!" Pete said, beaming. "I'm glad we could help the government."

"The Air Force Missile Test Center is grateful to you," Uncle Walt went on. "But of course the biggest mystery still remains unsolved—what happened to the missing nose cone. That three-million-dollar pay load is somewhere under water, I'm sure."

"You don't think it was blown to bits, Dad?" Randy asked.

"No. Some people have said this. But I put old Thuzzy's bonnet on myself, and it was well shielded from the LOX compartments."

"Then I'm going to play your hunch and keep on looking for it!" Pete exclaimed. "Uncle Walt, when we were looking for the cone in the Banana River, the wind blew our boat onto Cape Canaveral."

"What!"

"Sure, it was nothing," Ricky said, trying to look

very nonchalant. "We saw the submarine missile being fired."

Randy chuckled. "It didn't happen that easily, Dad." And the boys told their story.

When they had finished, their listeners looked amazed.

"You were unlucky and lucky at the same time," Mrs. Hollister said. "I'm sorry you didn't find the pay load but glad you saw a missile launching."

"I wish you'd caught the grandfather turtle!" Sue burst out. "I could have ridden on his back."

Everyone laughed, and Aunt Carol said, "I have some news too. Like to hear it?"

Pam looked at her aunt in surprise. "Was it something we did?"

"No, I heard this from one of the missile mothers," her aunt replied. "I thought I'd save the news until we were all together."

"Please, what is it?" Sharon begged.

"How would you all like to see an atomic submarine?"

"Oh, yes!" the children replied.

Aunt Carol said that one was coming into Port Canaveral next morning. "People are invited to look at the atomic sub," she said. "We can't go aboard, though."

For a moment Ricky looked disappointed. He said he could imagine getting into the sub and sailing under the North Pole!

"That would be a nice trip," Uncle Walt said.

Then he winked. "But don't forget, my young detectives, your work here isn't finished yet."

"We'll keep on sleuthing, Uncle Walt," Pete assured him. Aside, he whispered to Pam, "Port Canaveral ought to be a good place to look for clues."

"Oh, I do hope we can solve the mystery at Missile Town," Pam said fervently.

Much to the surprise of the Hollisters, they discovered next morning that Port Canaveral was a small harbor cut into the base of the Cape a short distance from the road leading to the missile range. As they alighted from the station wagon, the first thing the children noticed was a line of fishing boats moored beside a long dock.

"I guess those are shrimp boats," Holly remarked to Pam.

The craft looked like the kind the children had seen sailing in the sea off Cocoa Beach. They had tall masts with rigging. On the decks lay two wooden frames resembling doors, and at the stern of the boat was a huge pile of nets.

Moored beside the shrimp boats were several smaller craft, each with a roof extending over the open deck. At the four corners were large metal reels mounted on posts.

Pete wandered off ahead of the others, looking for the atomic sub. The boy approached a fisherman no taller than himself. The man wore boots, a rough sweater, and a skullcap.

"Can you tell me where to find the atomic submarine?" Pete asked him.

"It isn't in yet, son," the man replied.

"Are these shrimp boats?" Pete pointed.

"Yes, and the others are snapper boats," he answered.

The fisherman, who said his name was Shorty, offered to tell Pete about the fishing that went on at Cape Canaveral.

"Oh, thanks," Pete said. "But first let me call the others. They'd like to hear it too."

"Well," Shorty said, as the children and their mothers surrounded him, "I didn't know I'd have such a big audience as this."

He explained that the shrimp boats operated in a peculiar fashion.

"You see those two doors?" he asked, pointing to the deck of one of the boats.

"Oh, yes," Sue spoke up. "That's so the fish can get in and out."

"These doors work differently," Shorty said with a chuckle. He explained that the doors, both attached to the back of the boat by long ropes, were lowered parallel into the water. Between them stretched a chain, and behind the chain bellowed a huge shrimp net.

"As the doors and chain are dragged flat across the ocean floor," he said, "the chain disturbs the shrimp. They jump up and land in the net."

The fisherman went on to say that Canaveral shrimp were known far and wide.

"Um, are they delicious!" Sharon exclaimed.

"And so are the snappers," Aunt Carol added.

"Now that is the fish I like to catch," Shorty said. "Shrimp boats aren't for me. Too much net mending all the time."

Shorty told the children that catching snapper was real sport. Bait was put on the hooks and unreeled clear down to the ocean floor.

"The snapper lie in deep holes," he said. "That is where we catch them."

Shorty said the children might step onto the shrimp and snapper boats. The storm of the previous day had made the water too rough for profitable fishing this morning. "But we'll go out again early tomorrow," he said.

While Mrs. Hollister and Aunt Carol gazed across the harbor for a sign of the atomic submarine, all the children except Pete and Pam scampered about the decks of the shrimp and snapper boats. Pete and Pam followed Shorty and continued asking questions in low voices. "Do you know all the fishermen at Port Canaveral?" Pete lead off.

"Just about," the man replied, stroking his chin.

"Have you heard of one named Ferguson?" Pam inquired.

Shorty looked from one child to the other. "Can't say that I know him well. He's an odd duck."

"How do you mean?" Pete asked.

"Well, he and his crew don't talk to anyone," Shorty said. "They're unfriendly. Maybe that's because they come from the Gulf."

"You mean the Gulf of Mexico?" Pam interjected.

"Yes, that's where they came from a few months ago," Shorty went on. "I never saw anyone fish for shrimp like that crew does. At all hours of the day and night."

The children's hearts thumped with excitement. Here was something else strange about Alec Ferguson! Why had he brought his shrimp boat from the Gulf of Mexico? And why were he and his crew so unfriendly?

Shorty looked straight at Pete. "Why are you so interested in this fellow?" he asked.

Pete thought it best not to reveal too much, so he merely said, "Alec Ferguson doesn't like children. He chased us away from his shack. A missile man was there with him. Do you know who he is?"

Shorty said Ferguson was very friendly with one of his crew. He might be the one, but the fellow was no missile man. "I don't think he lives with Alec," Shorty went on, "but he might have been visiting."

Just then Pete and Pam heard their mother "yoo-hoo." They looked along the dock and saw her waving an arm and pointing to the harbor mouth.

"The sub must be coming in," Pete said.

He turned to call to the children aboard the boats, when suddenly they all heard Holly and Randy set up a terrific wailing.

"Goodness!" Pam exclaimed. "What's happened to them?"

The cries came from one of the shrimp boats. Pete and Pam rushed onto the deck while Ricky stood there laughing. "Ha, ha, I caught two big shrimp!" he cried gleefully.

"Oh, there are Holly and Randy!" Pam said. "Ricky, you're a meany," she added reproachfully.

The children were tangled under the edge of the nets. "Ricky threw it over us!" Holly cried out, struggling to free herself.

"Wait until I get you!" Randy said.

Pete and Pam quickly lifted the net from the two captives. Their hair was disheveled, and they looked as if someone had been playing ticktacktoe on their faces.

Ricky dashed across the small gangplank, with Holly and Randy racing after him. By the time they reached their mothers, the two "shrimp" had calmed down sufficiently not to bother Ricky.

"We were going to throw you in the water," Holly declared, "but we'll play a trick on you, so watch out."

As Mrs. Hollister and Aunt Carol used handkerchiefs to wipe the dirt from the faces of Holly and Randy, scores of onlookers gathered at the edge of the dock to witness the approach of the atomic submarine, which loomed in the distance like a gigantic whale. It docked on the far side of the channel.

"I caught two big shrimp!" Ricky cried gleefully.

"Isn't she a beauty?" Pete said, as the hatch opened and several officers climbed out.

Mrs. Hollister held Ricky tightly by the hand and said, "If I let you go I know you'll get into that submarine somehow!" she teased.

Holly wrinkled her nose at the red-haired boy. She was not soon to forget his prank.

After the crowd had looked for some time at the sleek gray submarine, they started to turn away, since drops of rain had begun to fall.

"Hurry to the car," Aunt Carol directed the children, "before you get wet."

Pete stopped to say good-by to Shorty, as the fisherman hurried to the shelter of his snapper boat.

"Maybe you'd like to come fishing with me tomorrow," Shorty suggested.

"Can the whole family come?" Pete asked.

"No, I have room for only two," the man replied. "How about you and your sister Pam coming?"

Pete hastened to his mother and asked her consent. Mrs. Hollister consented, provided Shorty would bring the children back the same day. The fisherman said he would.

"Be seeing you, Shorty!" Pete called out as the car pulled away.

Ricky gazed at the downpour on the windows. "Yikes!" he said, folding his arms and slumping in his seat, "what can we do here on a rainy day?"

"Oh, I know," Sharon said. "How about indoor roller skating?"

"A good idea," her mother said. Aunt Carol told the Hollisters about a rink nearby. It was open on the sides but had a roof overhead to keep out the rain. "Covered rinks are very popular in this part of Florida," she said.

At an intersection, where the causeway crossed Merritt Island, Aunt Carol pulled off to the side of the road in front of a large skating rink. Everyone hurried out of the car and into the shelter of the structure.

The children rented skates. Even little Sue joined in the fun as they went round and round the rink. Several other young skaters were there. Before long they were playing tag with the cousins. When they tired of this, Holly said, "Let's play snap the whip."

"Oh, good!" Ricky cried. "Who'll be the tail of the whip?"

"You!" Holly said with a wink at her cousin Randy.

The Hollister and Davis children joined hands, along with several other skaters. Ricky was at the end of the whip, holding Holly's hand. Pete skated in the lead. He stopped short and swung the rest of the skaters around in a wide arc.

Ricky, on the end, went faster and faster. "Hey! Help! Wait!" he called. "Holly, hold me tight!"

But Holly had other ideas. She let go of her brother's hand and Ricky sailed across the rink.

"Help!" he cried.

CHAPTER 13

A *SUSPICIOUS STRANGER*

RICKY skated right off the edge of the rink, flew through the air, and landed in a puddle of water.

"Oh, dear!" Mrs. Hollister said, hurrying to his side.

"Holly did it!" Ricky cried angrily.

"Oh, come now," his mother replied. "Aren't you the big boy who caught the two shrimp a while ago?"

This made Ricky laugh in spite of himself. Even though the seat of his pants was wet, no one remarked about this, and soon he was skating around the rink again.

"But there will be no more whip," Aunt Carol said.

When it was nearly time to leave, Pete glanced toward the road and saw Marshall Holt riding his bicycle. The boy had a slicker over his head. As he drew closer to the rink, he waved.

"Hey, Pete!" he called out, "I was just coming over to your house to see you about something."

"It must be important," Pete said, as he bent down to loosen his skates.

"I'll say it's important!" Marsh answered. He parked his bicycle alongside the rink and hastened up to the Hollister and Davis children. "I've been playing detective," he said, "and I've found some swell clues."

"What do you mean?" Pam asked.

Marsh said he had crept up beside Alec Ferguson's shack that morning. "I hid in the bushes so no one could see me, and guess what? I heard those two men talking."

"What did they say?" Randy asked.

"The words I heard were 'countdown,' 'T time,' and 'military secret.'"

"Crickets!" Pete exclaimed. "Maybe the men are spies!"

Pete recalled the security officer's remark that there had been prowlers on the missile base. Perhaps these were the men in question.

"It was fun playing detective," Marsh said proudly. "But kind of scary."

"You did a good job," Pete said, praising his new friend.

"Do you suppose we could do more sleuthing together at the shack, Pete?" Marsh asked.

"I'd like to."

"Then why don't you come to my house and stay overnight? I'd like to show you a pram I'm building."

"Good. Boats are a hobby of mine too. Let's work it out together this evening. This afternoon we'll go sleuthing."

Mrs. Hollister approved with a smile and said, "Don't get into any trouble."

"We'll be careful, Mother," Pete assured her.

The shower stopped and the sun shone down on the little puddles of water as the Hollisters and their cousins left the rink. Marsh suggested that he and Pete ride off on his bicycle.

"Okay, let's go," Pete said. Marsh told him to use the seat. He himself stood up on the pedals and pumped, steering the bicycle. The boys headed back toward Cocoa Beach, and the rest of the family drove to the Davis cottage.

Pete had never seen the Holts' home before. Marsh turned into a side street near the Cocoa Beach shopping center. He pedaled into the driveway of a pretty ranch-type house surrounded by flowering shrubs.

"Oh, Mom! Pete came with me!" Marsh called happily.

Mrs. Holt greeted the two boys in the living room. "I'm so glad you came, Pete," she said. "Marsh doesn't have many playmates near his own age!"

Mrs. Holt showed him the guest bedroom. "You'll find pajamas in the dresser," she said, "and a new toothbrush."

"Thank you," Pete said.

"Marsh is very interested in playing detective," his mother went on. "Do you really think suspicious-acting people live in the fisherman's shack?"

"Yes, I do," Pete replied. "But so far we have no positive proof they're up to anything dangerous."

"Let's go down there after lunch and watch," Marsh proposed.

"Okay. But right now I'd like to see your boat."

Marsh led Pete out to the carport beside the cottage. In the back of the open-air garage lay a partially built pram, supported by two sawhorses.

"Say, this is keen," Pete said as he examined the small boat.

"She'll hold two people and be great for fishing on the river," Marsh said proudly. "Will you help me put in some more screws?"

"Sure, after we've done our detecting."

"Luncheon is ready, boys!" Mrs. Holt called.

After eating hot soup, sandwiches, and homemade cream puffs, the boys rode to the beach. They got off the bicycle and propped it against a palm tree alongside the lane, then walked toward Alec Ferguson's place.

When the top of his shack came into sight over a low dune, Marsh said, "What shall we do now, Pete?"

"Make believe we're looking for shells."

The boys walked slowly, stooping now and then to pick up shells and examine them. Gradually Pete edged closer to the shack. As he did, the front door opened and a man stepped out.

Tall and stooped, like a blade of beach grass, the stranger walked with a swaying motion toward a nearby sand dune. He wore rough khaki trousers and a blue shirt, with sleeves rolled up over muscular arms. The man had a jutting chin, and the shock of black hair halfway down his forehead gave him a fierce look.

"Is that Alec?"

"No. Don't stare at him, Marsh."

The stranger seemed unaware of the two boys. Reaching the top of the dune, he pulled a spyglass from his pocket and held it up to his right eye.

Both boys were spellbound by the man's actions. If they suspected spies, this fellow certainly was acting the role. Now his telescope swept the ocean. Suddenly the glistening lens was pointed straight at the two boys.

"Golly!" Marsh cried in surprise. "He sees us."

Pete's throat felt tight and his cheeks flushed with embarrassment. They had forgotten to act like detectives! Standing there and staring at the stranger would certainly arouse his suspicions.

"Come on," Pete quickly said, "let's pretend to be doing something."

Suddenly Marsh gave Pete a hard shove, sending him sprawling on the sand.

"Hey! Oh, I get it. Great idea!"

Pete rose and lunged at Marsh, grasping the taller boy around the waist and pulling him down. The two rolled over and over away from the shack. When they finally stopped to look back, the stranger had disappeared.

"I hope he thought we were having a fight," Marsh said, brushing the sand from his trousers.

"He thinks we're really fighting," Marsh said.

"That was quick thinking, pal. Let's see where he went." Pete ran around the side of Alec Ferguson's place in time to see a car disappearing down the lane which led to the main road.

"He got away," Pete said, bending down to look at the tracks. "The car must have been parked here. I wonder if Alec went with him."

The boys quietly watched and listened, but there was no sign of activity from within the shack. "This leaves us with a suspicion," Marsh said with a sigh, "but no clues."

"Let's keep looking."

"Where?"

"Right here," Pete said. "This is the place where the man got into the car."

The hard-packed ground and stunted grass growing in the trough between the tire tracks revealed only a few dim footprints.

"If there are any clues, I can't see them," Marsh said.

"Say, what's this?" Pete asked. Stepping to the side of the drive, he bent down to pick up a small square of white paper, carefully folded.

"Is it a letter?" Marsh asked eagerly.

Pete opened it. The paper was blank.

"Oh, shucks!" Marsh said. "There goes a good clue!"

"Maybe not," Pete said. "Here, smell this." He held the paper to Marsh's nose.

"Onions. What does that mean?"

"Possibly invisible writing."

Pete had once learned from Police Officer Cal in Shoreham that onion juice could be used for invisible writing. When heated, the paper would reveal the words clearly.

"Let's take it home and see!" Marsh urged.

He pedaled fast again while Pete sat on the seat. They zipped along, skidding into the Marsh driveway.

"Goodness, what's the matter?" Mrs. Holt asked as the boys rushed in the house.

"We'd like a match, please," Pete said, and told what they had found. Mrs. Holt gave him one.

Pete struck it and carefully held the flame under the white paper to heat it. Gradually words appeared.

"Think you are on the right track.
Keep trying. Tomorrow may be the
day."

"You were right, Pete. But what does the message mean?"

"Those men are trying to do something undercover, whatever it is. And I'll bet it's illegal."

"Let's go back and find out," Marsh suggested, and they rode off again.

The boys left the bicycle in the same lane as before. But this time, instead of going onto the beach, they walked along the shore road, approaching Alec Ferguson's property from the road.

Pete and Marsh moved catlike among the palm trees and scraggly oaks, making certain to conceal themselves from direct view of the house. Finally Pete whispered, "Look! The car's back again."

"Is there anybody in it?"

"No," Pete answered. Then he said, "Listen!"

In the distance a loud voice said, "Get out!"

Marsh cringed and Pete was perplexed. "How do they know we're out here?" he whispered. "Do you suppose those men have some kind of warning system rigged up?"

Suddenly the boys felt two strong hands grab them by the backs of their necks. An icy voice said, "Now I've got you!"

CHAPTER 14

TRACKING A FAKER

Turning his head, Pete saw the dark-haired man they had observed scanning the sea with the telescope.

"I thought you'd come back," he said harshly, "so I was waiting for you."

"Who are you?" Pete asked, trying to shake himself free of the iron grip.

"I'll ask the questions, you young snoopers," their captor ordered. He spun both boys around to face him.

"Let me go!" Marsh cried. "I'll tell my father."

"You can tell him," the man said menacingly, "that you were trespassing on private property and that Mr. Turk taught you a lesson."

"We didn't mean any harm," Pete said. "There's something mysterious about Alec Ferguson's shack and we were trying to find . . ."

"Find what?"

"Who the missile man is who lives here."

"Yes," Marsh added. "Are you the one?"

Mr. Turk put his head back and laughed loudly. "So that's it! You're looking for a missile man. Well, there's none around here." He relaxed his grip and his voice became milder.

Mr. Turk said that there had been a number of thefts from cottages along the shore front, and that he thought the boys were up to some mischief.

"We wouldn't steal anything," Pete protested.

"I've seen you creeping around this place," Mr. Turk went on. "What were you doing?"

Pete explained that the monkey tracks had led his sister to the shack. "We found Lady Rhesus later," the boy added, without giving any further information.

"Then why didn't you vamoose after that?"

Pete hesitated to give the full answer. Mr. Turk could possibly be innocent of any wrongdoing, but, on the other hand, he might be acting. "Would you answer a few questions for us?" Pete asked.

Mr. Turk smiled. "Certainly. Of course."

"Where is your friend, Mr. Ferguson?"

"Out on his shrimp boat, fishing."

"Oh," Marsh broke in quickly. "Is that what you were looking at through the spyglass?"

"No," came the reply. "I was looking at the porpoises. I can tell by the way they jump whether tomorrow will be a good day for fishing."

"Why aren't you fishing today?" Pete asked.

"It's my day off." The stern look on the man's face now had vanished, and he spoke in a friendly tone. "Well, fellows, I can see it was all a mistake." He put a hand in his pocket. "How about us being friends? Be my guest and treat yourself to some ice cream."

He pulled out a dollar bill. At the same time a piece of paper fluttered to the ground. Pete bent over to pick it up. As he handed the paper to Mr. Turk, Pete noticed that a rectangular diagram was drawn on it.

"Thanks," the man said, and pressed the money into Marsh's hand.

"We can't take any money," Pete told Mr. Turk, and Marsh nodded agreement.

"Okay. Suit yourselves. But remember, don't sneak around this place any more."

The boys turned and hurried down the lane to the road. As they reached the bicycle, Marsh said, "What do you make of him, Pete?"

"He's a phony."

"I think so too. He was just trying to bribe us."

"And what's more," Pete said, "the diagram on that paper looked like a sketch of the laboratory building at Patrick that I saw at the Davises'."

"Golly! Shouldn't you have mentioned it to him?"

"No," Pete replied. "It would have aroused his suspicion of us even more. We'll let Turk think we didn't notice it, but I'm going to tell Uncle Walt."

On the way home, Marsh talked about the mysterious shack and wondered more than ever who had been inside, talking about missiles with Alec Ferguson.

"We don't know the whole story," Pete said; but he vowed he would find out before they left Cape Canaveral.

141

"Don't come around anymore," the gruff man said.

When they reached the Holt home, Marsh rushed to the telephone table, picked up a pencil, and wrote down a number. Proudly he showed it to Pete.

"What's this?"

"The license number of the car behind Ferguson's shack."

"Swell!" Pete exclaimed.

"I memorized it while you were asking the questions," Marsh said, grinning proudly.

At supper he showed his father the license number, and told him about their adventure.

"Hmm," Mr. Holt said. "This is a rented car. I can tell by the special serial numbers. Maybe I can find out something about this Turk fellow."

After several telephone calls, Marsh's father located the agency from which the car had been rented. Fortunately, the man who owned the agency was an old friend of his, and gladly told what he knew of Mr. Turk. When the conversation was over, Mr. Holt turned to the boys.

"There wasn't much I could learn about Turk. He's been here only a short time. Gave his home address as New Orleans. As reference he named a bank in that city."

"Which one?" Pete asked.

"The Dixie Trust Company."

"May we telephone the bank in the morning?" Pete asked. "I'll pay for it."

Mr. Holt said he would gladly pay for the telephone call, since it might reveal more about the suspected men. "And if the bank doesn't give him a good reference, you boys may be on a hot trail!"

Pete and Marsh relaxed from their strenuous day of sleuthing by working on the pram during the evening. Both boys used screw drivers until their wrists ached, but accomplished a great deal. By nine-thirty the bottom of the boat was securely put in place.

"Whew! Let's call it a day," Marsh said finally.

"Okay, skipper."

In spite of the exciting day, Pete slept without dreaming, and awakened early the next morning. At breakfast he looked up at the wall clock and said, "Marsh, will it ever get to be eight o'clock?"

"Only half an hour to go," his friend replied, "and we'll learn the facts about Mr. Turk."

Pete put through the call to the New Orleans bank. In answer to his query, the bank official looked up Mr. Turk's records. "Sorry," came the voice over the long-distance wire, "we have no record of a Mr. Turk."

"Thanks," Pete said, and hung up. "Crickets, Marsh! That guy really *is* a phony!"

"Let's call the police," Marsh suggested.

"Wait a second," Pete said. "Remember Mr. Jeep? He's a retired policeman and a special deputy. I'll call him."

Luckily they found their friend at his home.

"You've been persistent about that shack and its occupants," Mr. Jeep told Pete. "You may have uncovered a big puzzle here. Leave it to me."

144

"I'll have to," Pete said, "because Pam and I are going snapper fishing this morning."

Mr. Jeep told Pete that he would first notify the car-rental company, which apparently had not bothered to check on the man's reference. Then he would do some sleuthing himself.

Shortly afterward, Mrs. Holt and Marsh drove Pete to Port Canaveral. As the car turned onto the docks, Marsh said, "I wish I were going with you. I've never been snapper fishing."

"Maybe Shorty will take you someday," Pete said. "Oh, here comes the Davises' station wagon."

Aunt Carol waved as she drove up next to the Holts' car. Seated beside her was Pam, dressed in a cotton knit shirt and dungarees. In the back seat sat Ricky, with Missy on his lap.

When everyone stepped from the cars, Pete introduced the two women, Pam, and Ricky. "My niece and nephew should have a lot of fun fishing today," Aunt Carol remarked.

"But what about me?" Ricky asked glumly, as Missy frisked around his feet.

"Oh, you'll find some kind of adventure," his aunt said, laughing.

Pete quickly located Shorty's boat, the *Zephyr*, but the snapper fisherman had not yet arrived. Berthed not far from the *Zephyr* was a lone shrimp boat, rocking gently. Four men busied themselves on its deck. Almost at once, Pete recognized two of them as Ferguson and Turk.

"Pam, Ricky," Pete said quietly, "come over here." Concealed behind Mrs. Holt's car, Pete told them about his new suspicion. "Maybe we'll have time to learn something more about these two men," he added.

Because Ricky was not known to the pair on the shrimp boat, it was decided that he should do the sleuthing.

"Walk right up to the boat," Pete instructed him, "and act as if you're just curious. Listen to everything they're saying."

Ricky was keen for the job. "Here I go!" he said enthusiastically. He whistled for Missy, who was sniffing at a fish head near the dock's edge.

Together boy and dog made their way casually toward the shrimp boat. Now Ricky was close enough to read the name *Gulf Storm* on the bow.

Mrs. Holt and Aunt Carol were chatting beside the station wagon, unaware of the children's plans. Pete, Pam, and Marsh sauntered toward Shorty's craft, watching Ricky intently.

"He's doing great so far," Marsh observed as Ricky stood beside the gunwale of the *Gulf Storm*, rocking on his heels and gazing at the pile of nets.

Ferguson and Turk were talking together in front of the cabin. The latter glanced up at Ricky and scowled but said nothing.

Just then Pam, who had been watching closely, sucked in her breath. "Oh!" she cried softly. "Look!"

Missy had climbed to the low railing of the boat,

poised on her short, stubby legs. She balanced herself for a few moments, swaying to the motion of the boat. Ricky whistled and called, "Come here, Missy!"

But the dachshund did not obey. Instead she leaped forward like a flying sausage and landed on the pile of nets.

"Hey!" Scram!" Alec Ferguson cried.

"Get that dog out of here before we shove off!" Turk ordered one of the crew.

The man started toward the nets and reached over to grab Missy. The dog yelped and panicked, struggling to jump clear of the tangled strands, but instead she became hopelessly ensnared in the shrimp nets.

"Don't hurt our dog!" Ricky cried, and jumped aboard the vessel.

"Get that kid out of here too!" Turk yelled.

Ferguson made a lunge for Ricky, but tripped over a rope and landed on the deck with a thud. Ricky darted out of his reach and stopped at the steps leading to the cabin.

For an instant Ricky glimpsed a shiny array of gadgets that looked like the works of a giant television set.

Now his eyes darted to Alec Ferguson, who had risen and was pursuing him again. Ricky leaped out of the way in time and scampered toward Missy, who was whining and yapping as two men tried to untangle her.

"You're hurting her!" he cried out.

"Get rid of that kid!" Turk bellowed.

Poor Ricky did not know what to do. He wanted to save Missy. But he had to escape from the angry men before the *Gulf Storm* started away from the dock.

By this time, Aunt Carol, Mrs. Holt and the other children, attracted by the commotion, had run to the side of the shrimp boat.

"Leave that boy and the dog alone!" Aunt Carol cried out.

"Come here, Ricky!" Pam screamed.

Her brother dodged around the cabin and leaped onto the dock just as Ferguson untied the mooring ropes. With the roar of the boat's engine, the *Gulf Storm's* propeller sent foam billowing at the stern and moved away from the dock.

Missy was still tangled in the nets.

"Stop! Give us our dog!" Pam wailed.

CHAPTER 15

THE FUNNY WARNING

IN SPITE of the children's cries, the *Gulf Storm* continued on its way out of Port Canaveral. The two crewmen continued to tug at Missy and finally freed the dachshund from the shrimp nets.

They handed the dog to Turk. With one sweep of his right arm, the man flung Missy into the water!

"Oh!" Pam screamed.

Missy disappeared for a few moments; then her long brown snoot came to the surface. The dog started to paddle furiously toward the dock.

"She's too far out! Missy will never make it!" Pam cried.

"Oh, our poor little dog!" Aunt Carol said woefully.

Just then Shorty drove onto the dock and hurried over to Pete. "What happened?" he asked.

Pete pointed to the tiny brown bundle struggling in the water.

"Come, I have a rowboat," Shorty said. He hurried to the *Zephyr*, with Pete and Pam running behind him. A dinghy for two passengers bobbed in the water behind the snapper boat.

"Hop in," Shorty commanded, bending over to

hold the small craft steady. Pete and Pam jumped in to the boat and each quickly took an oar while Shorty untied the line.

The others had now hastened to watch. "Hurry! Hurry!" Ricky called out as the oars splashed.

All this while Missy had been struggling to keep her head above water. Now she seemed confused and started to swim in circles.

Pete and Pam rowed out swiftly and soon came alongside their cousins' pet. Pete reached over the side, grabbed Missy's collar, and hauled her aboard. The little dog shivered and whimpered. As Pam cuddled her, she could feel the dog's heart pounding.

"Oh, you poor thing," she said. Pam moved to the back of the dinghy while Pete manned the oars. In a few minutes the boat was tied up and Missy was safely on the dock again.

What a fuss everyone made over her! The pet seemed to enjoy all the attention and ran about, barking and jumping at Aunt Carol.

"Those terrible men will hear from me the next time I see them!" Aunt Carol declared.

"We'd better start off now if we want to do any fishing," Shorty said. "Is my crew ready?"

"Aye, skipper," Pete said, saluting smartly.

"I'm ready too," Pam added, smiling.

"Here come the rest of my crew," Shorty announced, as three men dressed in boots and rough clothes drove up in an old, battered car.

"Good-by and good luck," Aunt Carol said.

Marsh slapped Pete on the back in farewell. "I hope you catch a whopper!"

"I'll settle for the nose cone," Pete said with a laugh.

He and Pam climbed aboard the *Zephyr*, and soon the snapper boat was steaming into the open waters of the Atlantic. Marsh, Ricky, and the two women waved until the craft was far out. Then they returned to their cars and drove home.

Missy had thoroughly recovered from her frightening swim by the time Aunt Carol pulled up in front of her cottage.

"Oh, look," Ricky said as he stepped out, "there's Mr. Jeep's jeep. He must be in the house."

Whitey was lolling in the shade of the car, and Missy soon made friends with the fluffy dog. They raced around the lawn together while Ricky and his aunt entered the house.

"We have company," Mrs. Hollister remarked as they came into the living room.

Mr. Jeep, seated in a comfortable overstuffed chair, rose to greet them.

"We had a big adventure!" Ricky declared and told the story of the happening at Port Canaveral.

"Did you ever hear of such cruel men!" Mrs. Hollister said.

"Cruel is right," Mr. Jeep said. He revealed that, after consulting the police chief, he had been assigned to investigate the fisherman's shack. "I thought those fellows were harmless," he said, "but

I think you children have unmasked some real villains."

"Yikes!" Ricky cried.

Mr. Jeep explained that he had hoped to speak with Pete and Pam before they set off on their fishing trip. "But I think I have enough information already," he said. "I'll go over and take a look at that place right away."

"May I go with you?" Ricky begged.

"Me too!" Holly said.

Little Sue climbed into Mr. Jeep's lap and looked up into his face. "You'll take me, please?"

Randy and Sharon looked glum and did not say a word.

Their mother knew what they were thinking. "I know you would like to join Mr. Jeep too," she said, "but you both have music lessons in an hour."

"I know, Mother," Randy said obediently, and Sharon bobbed her head in agreement.

Mr. Jeep looked at Mrs. Hollister for advice and said with a chuckle, "I know that all these young detectives want to help me, but it might be dangerous."

"We'll be careful!" Ricky said. "Won't we, Holly?"

"All right then," their mother said. "Ricky and Holly may go with you, Mr. Jeep, but Sue must stay here."

At first the little girl's chin began to quiver. Then

she burst out crying. "Little—little—detectives—miss all the fun!" she wailed. "I want to go too!"

Just then there came a light knock on the door and Miss Mott walked in with Lady Rhesus seated on her shoulder.

"My goodness, has something terrible happened?" the artist asked, seeing Sue's tears. The monkey jumped down from her shoulder, ran across the floor, and leaped into Sue's arms. Mrs. Hollister explained the cause of Sue's tears.

Miss Mott smiled. "Sue, I'm sure you'd have more fun at home being a monkey sitter."

The little girl immediately stopped crying and looked up with wide eyes. "Is a monkey sitter like a baby sitter?" she asked.

"Exactly," Miss Mott replied. "I have to leave town for a few days to attend an art show and thought you children might like to take care of Lady Rhesus."

Sue climbed down from Mr. Jeep's lap. With the monkey clinging to her back, she ran to Miss Mott and threw her arms about the woman.

"I'll love to be a monkey sitter, Miss Mott!" she said.

"And," Aunt Carol added, "you may have the space monkey all to yourself for a few hours."

Now that Sue was satisfied, Holly and Ricky kissed their mother good-by and left the house with Mr. Jeep. The car whizzed over the causeway toward

"You'll have more fun being a monkey-sitter."

Cocoa Beach. Mr. Jeep drove directly onto the sand and parked close to Alec Ferguson's shack.

"Now, you children stand back until I learn if there's any danger," he directed, and strode over the dunes toward the fisherman's house. He knocked sharply on the front door.

"Go away! Get out!" came a voice from inside.

Mr. Jeep identified himself as a deputy and said, "I want to speak to you."

There was no answer.

"What are you going to do now, Mr. Jeep?" asked Ricky. He and Holly were standing off to one side, holding hands.

"I'll have to go in and get him, whoever he is," Mr. Jeep said with determination.

While the two Hollister children watched, goggle-eyed, the deputy went to a side window. It was closed. Mr. Jeep hastened to his car and returned with a screw driver. In no time at all he was prying the window open. As he did, a buzzing noise came from inside the shack.

"What's that—a burglar alarm?" Ricky asked.

"I wonder," Mr. Jeep said as he climbed inside. A moment later he stuck his head out the window. "There's nobody in here!" he told the children.

Just then the voice said, "Countdown. T time." This was followed by two long whistles.

Mr. Jeep whirled around as the children ran up to the window. Standing on tiptoe, he and Holly looked into the room. Nobody was in sight.

"Well, I'll be a sandpiper's uncle!" the ex-policeman exclaimed. "Would you look at this!" He walked across the room to where a bird cage suspended on top of an iron stand stood in the shadows. In the cage was a black bird.

As Mr. Jeep approached it, the bird opened its beak and said, "Get out! Go away! Countdown! Scrub that bird!"

Holly and Ricky gasped in amazement. "It's a talking bird!" Holly cried out.

CHAPTER 16

A STRANGE CATCH

HOLLY and Ricky stared through the window in astonishment at the strange black talking bird.

"Is that a crow?" Ricky asked.

"No. It's a myna bird," Mr. Jeep replied. "My grandmother had one like it. You can always tell a myna by the white marking on its head."

The man looked around to find what was making the buzzing noise. Finally he saw an electric switch near the door. "This must be it," he said. "A burglar alarm. Why would Ferguson want such a thing?" At the turn of the switch, the noise stopped.

Mr. Jeep climbed back out of the window and joined the children. "I can't arrest a bird for not letting me in," he said sheepishly.

Ricky and Holly also felt embarrassed. "And all the time we thought it was a man talking," Holly said, shaking her head so hard her pigtails bounced.

The children returned to the car with Mr. Jeep. As they climbed in beside him, he frowned. "I still can't believe that those fellows aren't mixed up in something that's not entirely honest," he said.

"That's right," said Holly. "Remember the black feather that Lady Rhesus had in her paw when we found her on the beach? That must have come from the myna bird!"

"Then the monkey was in the fisherman's house after all!" Ricky exclaimed. "It wasn't honest to keep her."

"I'll take you home and then report everything to the police chief," Mr. Jeep declared. "The next move will be up to them."

"Please tell us more about myna birds," Holly said as they pulled on to the main road and started toward the long causeway leading to Cocoa.

Mr. Jeep told them that wild myna birds were found in India and parts of southern Asia. Ancient people, learning that the birds could imitate human speech, trained them as pets. "But I never heard a bird with such a deep voice as the one we just saw," the man admitted.

Even though the mystery of the strange voice had been solved, all agreed that the shrimp fisherman had acted very strangely.

When they arrived at the Davis house, Mr. Jeep let the two children off and drove back to Cocoa Beach. Excitedly, Ricky and Holly told their mother and Aunt Carol about the myna bird.

"It seems mysterious," Mrs. Hollister said, "that it should have been taught missile talk."

At that very moment Pete and Pam were talking with Shorty on the snapper boat. They had left Port Canaveral far behind and now were rolling over the ocean waves, nearly out of sight of the Florida shore.

"How do you know where to fish?" Pete asked. "Can you find snappers everywhere?"

Shorty explained that modern fishing was done scientifically. "Come into the cabin and I'll show you the fathometer," he said.

Pete and Pam followed him down a short flight of stairs into a small room. It was filled with all kinds of supplies and charts, and in one corner stood an instrument with a round glass face.

"This is a sonic depth finder," Shorty said. "It tells us how deep the water is where we are. Look here."

A small dot of light moved a gauge up and down, and numbers alongside it indicated that the sea bottom was ten fathoms below.

"That's sixty feet," Pete said. "Plenty deep."

The children recalled that snappers lay in deep holes on the bottom of the sea. Shorty went on, "When the depth finder shows us where a hole is, we fish there."

The fisherman added that some of the larger commercial fishing boats had depth finders which actually indicated the presence of fish swimming down below. "It works like radar," he said.

Just then the point of light dipped. "There's a hole," Pete said. "Are you going to stop here?"

"Right." Shorty called to the man at the wheel. The boat stopped and turned around until it was directly over the hole.

The lines on the four corner posts were already baited, and the lead weights carried them far down into the depths. Each of the fishermen held the slack line loosely in his fingers. Shorty's line jiggled. With a quick move he set the hook, then began reeling in. At the same time the three other men got strikes.

Soon the lines began dropping plump snappers onto the deck. They squirmed and wriggled until they were taken off the hooks.

Pete was about to ask if he might try his luck, when suddenly he saw a boat on the horizon. From its rigging he identified it as a shrimper.

"Pam," he said, "do you suppose that's Ferguson?"

Overhearing this remark, Shorty said, "There's a pair of binoculars in the cabin. Get them and take a look."

Pete hurried for the glasses. Then, steadying his elbows on the rail, he trained the binoculars on the distant boat, which was headed in their direction.

"What do you see?" Pam asked.

"It's a shrimp boat all right, but I can't see the men on board."

"Let me look," Pam requested.

"Okay." Pete handed her the glasses, and his sister studied the oncoming craft as Shorty and his crew flipped a few more snappers onto the deck.

"Here, Pete," the fisherman called, "give us a hand and toss the fish into this locker while we move on to another hole." He opened a long rectangular

"It's the mystery shrimp boat all right."

box that had ice in the bottom. Pete sprang to the task and began to throw the slippery fish into the box.

His sister's eyes were still fixed on the shrimp boat. "Pete," she said finally, "it's the *Gulf Storm*. And I can make out the men now."

"What are they doing?"

"Alec Ferguson has a telescope, and he's looking at us."

"Oh-oh!" said Pete. "I wonder if he thinks we're following him."

The snapper hole had been fished out, and now the entire catch lay in the bottom of the ice chest. Pete wiped his hands on a towel hanging near the cabin door and took the glasses again.

"Turk is looking at us now," he said. Pete observed that the *Gulf Storm* had turned slightly and was running parallel to the *Zephyr*. He reported this to Shorty, who was again studying the depth finder.

"I wonder what those coots are up to," the fisherman said. "This area is too deep for shrimp."

Pete's eyes were on the sonic finder. Suddenly he saw the light jump sharply. "Shorty!" he called out. "We just went over a bump."

"That's odd," the fisherman replied.

He called to the pilot to turn around. The bow slapped the waves as the *Zephyr* reversed its course. Shorty studied the instrument. Again the dot of light jumped.

"What do you make of it?" Pete asked.

"Maybe there's an old sunken hull of a ship beneath us," Shorty said.

"Could it be part of the missile that blew up?" Pam questioned.

Shorty said he did not think so. Government ships had scanned the area after the missile's failure. They had even dragged the bottom and sent divers down to look for debris.

"But they might have missed it," Pete said.

"See this," Shorty said. "Another hole. I'm glad you made us turn about, Pete."

Again the hooks were let down. Once more snappers tugged at the bait and were promptly snagged and hauled up.

"May Pam and I fish now?" Pete asked.

"Sure," Shorty replied. "You'll find a couple of extra poles in the cabin."

The children hastily found the equipment and baited the hooks. Then, standing in the bow of the *Zephyr*, they let the lines sink to the bottom.

Pete got the first bite. The fish fought furiously at the end of his line, and Pam had to help pull the snapper aboard.

"What a beauty!" Pete said, and ran to show it to Shorty.

Pam, meanwhile, had picked up her pole, which she had laid down in order to help Pete. Suddenly the line became taut and the pole bent under the weight of the catch.

"Pete! I've caught something big!" his sister cried. Pam tried to reel in, but the weight on the other end of the line was too much for her slender wrists.

"Let me help you," Pete offered. But he made little progress; in fact, the pole bent even more as he tugged.

"Crickets!" Pete exclaimed. "You've caught a monster, Pam!"

"Oh, Pete, maybe it's another turtle, like the one that pulled Ricky out of the rowboat."

"This one's not going to get away!" Pete strained with all his might to raise whatever it was that Pam had hooked on the ocean floor.

Crack! The pole split and the line went slack.

Before Pete got over his surprise, Shorty had sprung to his side and grabbed the pole. The line pulled in easily, so he handed the pole back to Pete.

"Oh!" Pam said, disappointed. "The monster got away."

"What do you think it was, Shorty?" Pete asked.

"Probably a shark, or a giant grouper."

"I'm terribly sorry it broke the pole," said Pete.

"We'll pay for it," Pam offered.

"Don't worry about that," Shorty said kindly. "The pole was old and probably dried out. No great loss to me." The fisherman returned to his reel.

Pete continued to pull in the line until the big hook came to the surface. It was badly bent, and caught in the barb was a small coil of wire. A puzzled expression crossed the children's faces as he removed the wire.

"It wasn't a fish I hooked after all," said Pam. Then she asked excitedly, "Pete! Do you suppose we snagged the nose cone?"

"Sh! Not so loud! We mustn't let anybody know about this but the missile men." Pete carefully folded his handkerchief around the wire and put it in his pocket. The children's hearts thumped with excitement. How they wished they could fly to Uncle Walt and give him the clue!

Pam bent close to her brother's ear. "We'll have to hurry back. If that really was the nose cone—— Oh, Pete, I feel all fluttery."

The children had been so busy the past few minutes that they had momentarily forgotten about the shrimp boat. Now Pam took a deep breath of the salty air and looked out over the sparkling water. What she saw made her gasp. "Pete! Alec Ferguson's boat is coming this way."

"It must have circled around us." The boy shielded his eyes and watched the *Gulf Storm* as it bobbed in the troughs of the blue-green waves. The men on deck were plainly visible now. One of them was looking through the telescope.

Seeing this, Pam had a frightening thought. Had the men on the shrimp boat seen Pete take the wire from the hook and hide it in his handkerchief? If so, would they too think of the lost nose cone and find it?

As the Hollisters watched, the *Gulf Storm* bore down on the *Zephyr*. Pam was frightened. "Pete! They're going to ram us!"

CHAPTER 17

SHADOWED

SUDDENLY the shrimp boat veered off and circled around the *Zephyr*. Shorty was annoyed. "Get away from here!" he cried out, waving his arms. "We want to fish."

But the *Gulf Storm* kept going round and round them. Pete and Pam grew more worried all the time. "They're trying to make us leave here," Pete told his sister.

"Perhaps we'd better go," Pam suggested. "The sooner we give Uncle Walt this wire we found, the better."

The Hollisters told Shorty that they wanted to be taken back to Port Canaveral. He readily agreed, saying that Ferguson's odd behavior would make snapper fishing impossible. "Besides," he added, "we have a fair catch now."

Shorty headed the *Zephyr* back toward shore, leaving the *Gulf Storm* far in the distance. Arriving at the dockside, Pete and Pam thanked the fisherman and ran to a public telephone booth at the end of the pier. Pete first dialed the Davises' home, in order to get his uncle's telephone number. Mrs. Hollister was surprised to find that the children had returned so soon, and told them about the myna bird.

"Crickets!" Pete exclaimed. "How about that!" Then he related what had happened on the sea and asked for Uncle Walt's telephone number at Cape Canaveral.

After receiving this, Pete hung up and called his uncle's office on the missile base.

"Mr. Davis is very busy," a secretary replied. "He can't be reached for at least half an hour."

When Pete told Pam of this and of the myna-bird incident, she became nervous. There was no time to by wasted. But without Uncle Walt, they might not be able to get into the laboratory at Patrick Air Force Base with the coil of wire.

"We'll just have to wait," Pete said, striding up and down the dock.

"But suppose Alec Ferguson's boat comes in and they chase us," Pam said. The shrimp boat, however, still was a small dot on the horizon.

Ten minutes passed. Then the children heard a rumbling and saw a bright flash in the sky.

"Missile! Missile!" Pam cried.

A long rocket reached toward outer space, waving a trail of orange flame as if saying good-by to earth for the last time.

Pete and Pam craned their necks until the missile was out of sight. Then Pete said with a grin, "Thuzzy rides again! No wonder we couldn't get Uncle Walt. He must have been busy getting his bird ready."

Pam ran into the booth to telephone again. This time the call reached her uncle.

"Hello, Pam," he said cheerfully. "Did you see the shoot?"

"Yes, Pete and I are at Port Canaveral."

"Then you had a good view. Thuzzenelda may not come back to earth for a million years, if ever." He paused. "What's on your mind, honey?"

Pam whispered into the phone, "I think we've found another clue."

"Where?"

"In the ocean." Pam quickly told him about the coil of wire.

"Stay where you are," Uncle Walt said. "I'll drive right over."

Fifteen minutes later the missile man arrived in the Bug, still wearing the hard hat used by people working around the gantries. "Let's see the wire, Pete," he said as the boy opened the car door for him.

Pete handed his uncle the handkerchief, which the missile man opened carefully. After studying the coil for a moment he said, "Pam, you may have hooked a three-million-dollar fish. I'll take this to the lab immediately. Hop in!"

As the Bug headed south along the highway, Uncle Walt passed one car after another to make time. When they reached Cocoa Beach, Pete glanced through the rear window. A red and white car was right behind them, keeping up to the Bug as the small automobile threaded its way through the traffic. The man at the wheel wore a round white badge.

"Uncle Walt, is that car following us on purpose?" Pete asked.

"It looks that way."

"Is he a policeman?"

"No. He appears to be a reporter. Probably hurrying to Patrick for the latest information about the bird we just fired."

As Pete and Pam looked back, the man smiled, and once waved to Pam, who felt embarrassed and turned around, blushing.

A mile north of the entrance to Patrick Air Force Base, the line of traffic slowed to a halt. Uncle Walt leaned out of the window and looked ahead.

"A road repair!" he said impatiently. "This *would* happen when we're in a hurry."

As the line of cars inched along, Pete saw a roller flattening a newly laid stretch of blacktop. North and south traffic was being detoured by a policeman over a sandy strip alongside the highway. Seeing his uncle grip the wheel nervously, Pete offered to run ahead and tell the officer of their predicament.

"Okay, Pete. Try it."

The boy stepped out and ran along the line of cars until he reached the officer, who wore the uniform of the military police. Pete told him that his uncle was going to the base on urgent business.

"Right, young fellow," the policeman said. "I'll see that he gets there in a hurry." The officer blew his whistle and stopped both lines of traffic. Then he beckoned to Uncle Walt to drive directly through the detour. The man behind him followed too.

"Thanks," Uncle Walt said, saluting the officer as he stopped to pick up Pete. Thinking the two cars were together, the traffic policeman waved them both on their way.

"That fellow had a nerve following us," Pam said.

"Reporters usually do," Uncle Walt said, chuckling.

Shortly after the Bug drove through the main gate, the car following disappeared down a side street of the sprawling base. Mr. Davis found a parking spot behind the laboratory building and stepped out of the car.

"Wait here for me," he said, and with a wink added, "Don't play with the horn."

"I won't," Pete promised, and watched his uncle hasten across the walk and disappear inside the laboratory building.

While Pete and Pam waited, they talked about the surprise Holly and Ricky had had when Mr. Jeep investigated Ferguson's shack. Where had the myna bird learned his missile language? they wondered.

"Maybe the bird once belonged to a missile man," Pam said, "and Ferguson used it to frighten children away from his place."

"But what about Lady Rhesus?" Pete pondered. "Alec Ferguson must have held the monkey for some reason."

"That fellow had a nerve following us."

The invisible-writing note was the most puzzling riddle of all, they agreed. If something was going to happen this very day, what could it be? Pete wondered whether the strange action of the *Gulf Storm* and her crew had anything to do with the answer to this question.

"Maybe we never will learn all the facts," Pam said with a sigh. "But I do hope Uncle Walt will have good luck in the lab."

Suddenly Pam glanced out the window on her side of the car and gasped, "Oh, Pete!"

"What's the matter?"

"That man who followed us."

Hearing Pam's exclamation, the stranger, who had been squatting beside the right rear wheel, quickly stood up. He smiled at the brother and sister, all the while fingering his press badge.

"Hello, there," he said. "Sorry to frighten you." He leaned into the window. "Your tire appeared soft, so I bent down to look at it."

"Is it getting flat?" Pete asked.

"No. It's all right." The man cleared his throat. "My name's Bittley. I'm on the St. Louis *Record*. Reporter, you know."

"I can see that by your badge," Pete said. "Did you follow us all the way from Port Canaveral?"

"Matter of fact, I did," Mr. Bittley said smoothly.

Pete felt uncomfortable under the fellow's gaze. His close-set eyes darted from Pete to Pam and back again.

"Are you looking for Mr. Davis?" Pam asked the man, who seemed reluctant to leave.

"I was looking for you." Mr. Bittley gave a nervous laugh and continued, "Tell me about the big fish you nearly caught. It will make a good feature story for my newspaper."

Something about the man's actions made Pete suspicious. He tried to change the subject. "Why aren't you reporting the missile shoot, Mr. Bittley?"

"Oh, that was routine. Minor, in fact. Now tell me about the fish. How near the surface was it when it got away?" He addressed the question to Pam and stared at her.

"How did you learn about that?" the girl countered.

"Shorty told me just as you were leaving," he said. "And what about that other thing you hooked?"

"We gave it to Uncle——" Pam bit her lip, fearing that she had said too much.

"And he took it to the laboratory?" Mr. Bittley went on.

"We're not going to tell you any more," Pete said, flushing.

He knew that Shorty had not said anything about the wire, because he had not seen it. This man was obviously lying. He must be connected in some way with Ferguson, Turk, and their crew, Pete thought. Should he try to get rid of Mr. Bittley, or hold the man in conversation until Uncle Walt came back?

Before Pete could make a decision, his uncle

dashed out of the laboratory building. Mr. Bittley saw him and hurried off, disappearing among the cars in a parking lot across the street.

Smiling broadly, Mr. Davis ran to the Bug and slid behind the wheel. "Children, you've discovered it!" he exclaimed.

"The nose cone?" Pete cried.

"Yes. The Air Force is starting a new search for it right away—and we're going to help."

Pete and Pam were so excited they could hardly talk. As their uncle started the Bug, Pete told the story of the curious Mr. Bittley.

"He knows it was the nose cone too! What'll we do, Uncle Walt?"

The missile man said there was no time to look for Bittley, who, he agreed, must be an impostor and not a reporter. "The police will pick him up later, I'm sure," he said. "We have to get to Port Canaveral in a hurry."

Uncle Walt drove fast toward the main gate. As he turned onto the highway, the three passengers were startled by a loud *bang*.

The Bug skidded onto the sandy shoulder of the road and turned on its side!

CHAPTER 18

YOUNG HEROES

INSIDE the wrecked car Pete and Pam lay in a jumble of arms and legs.

"Pete! Uncle Walt! Are you all right?" Pam cried, struggling to her feet.

The missile man, with a small cut on his forehead, pushed open the door. "I'm okay. How about you?"

"Just tangled up a bit," Pete said. "I'll bet that Bittley was responsible for this."

Uncle Walt hoisted himself out, then helped his niece and nephew from the car. By this time several passing vehicles, including a blue military-police car, had stopped to investigate the accident.

A sergeant carrying a first-aid kit hurried up to Uncle Walt and quickly bandaged his forehead. "That was a close call," he said. "How did it happen?"

"Sabotage," Pete said. "Look at the right rear tire."

The policeman, along with Uncle Walt and several bystanders, lifted the Bug onto its four wheels. The officer bent down to examine the tire.

"You're right. There's a deep slash on the inside wall. It caused a blowout as you made the turn onto the highway."

Pam told the officer about Mr. Bittley. "I'm sure he did this to keep us from getting back to Port Canaveral," she stated.

Uncle Walt took the policeman aside and explained the situation.

"Then there's no time to change the tire," the officer said. "Come with me. I'll take you to the port."

Uncle Walt, Pete, and Pam climbed into the military-police car. With siren wailing to clear the road in front of them, the automobile raced north through Cocoa Beach.

During the speedy ride, the officer radioed a description of Mr. Bittley and asked both the military and local police to be on the lookout for the man.

When the officer pulled into Port Canaveral, the harbor was bustling with activity. Two fast launches were on their way out to the open sea; a large helicopter hovered overhead, and a score of uniformed officers stood beside the *Zephyr*, talking with Shorty and his crew.

A tall, broad-shouldered man wearing captain's bars on his tunic separated himself from the group and strode over to meet Uncle Walt and the Hollisters.

"Operation Pickup is under way, Mr. Davis," he said. "I've sent two boats out to the spot where these children hooked onto the missing pay load." He extended a hand to Pete and Pam. "I'm Captain Nolan. Congratulations for your great discovery."

After shaking hands with the handsome captain, they told of their suspicions regarding the shrimp boat and its crew.

"They were well founded," Captain Nolan said, "and your sleuthing excellent. We've already caught Bittley."

"Great!" Pete exclaimed. "Where did you find him?"

"Our men caught him just after he entered Ferguson's shack. Your friend Mr. Jeep tipped us off to his possible whereabouts. But that's not all."

The security captain said that Bittley had been nabbed in a secret room under the shack while sending a radio message to the *Gulf Storm* by means of a powerful set.

"Bittley was an impostor, as you guessed," he praised the children. "He admitted cutting your uncle's tire, but he hasn't told us the full story yet."

As the captain spoke, the helicopter landed on the dockside, not far from where the group was standing. When the twin rotors whined to a halt, a smiling young lieutenant stepped out.

"We're ready, Captain," he said, saluting. "There's room enough for everybody, including Mr. Davis and the Hollisters."

"Thank you, Lieutenant." Captain Nolan called to Shorty, "You're invited too. We want all the help possible."

The Hollisters grinned at each other in sheer delight, and preceded Uncle Walt and Shorty into the cabin of the helicopter.

"Crickets, Pam! Isn't this keen?" Pete said, settling himself into one of the bucket seats.

"Oh, I hope we find the pay load before Ferguson and Turk do," Pam said, as the rotors whirred into life again.

The copter leaped into the air as if a giant missile were towing it skyward, and headed over the water. Soon Port Canaveral looked like a tiny picture postcard in the distance.

"We should be over the location in a few minutes," said Captain Nolan, who was seated across the aisle from Pete and Pam. "Our boats are there now, and we expect a report momentarily." He arose, walked to the cockpit, and talked to the pilot.

Pam, meanwhile, peered through the little window beside her. "Look, Pete!" she cried over the racket of the motors. "I can see the speedboats now."

The two craft were circling in choppy waves over the place where Pam had made her catch.

"Their instruments should pick up the nose cone easily," Uncle Walt said as the helicopter hung motionless over the boats.

Captain Nolan returned from the cockpit, a frown creasing his forehead. "Shorty," he said, "are you sure this is the right spot?"

The fisherman replied that to the best of his recollection this was the area where the depth finder had showed the bump on the ocean floor.

"My men can't locate a thing," Captain Nolan said, puzzled. "I've told them to widen their circle."

The officer returned to the pilot, and the boats circled ever wider. He returned again, looking more worried than before. "Something's gone wrong. Our finders can't see anything down there but fish."

"Maybe the shrimp boat found it," Pete declared.

The captain stroked his chin thoughtfully. "Did you children see any diving equipment on the *Gulf Storm?*" Neither had, and said so, but Pam added, "Couldn't they have fished up the nose cone in their nets?"

"That may be the answer!" Captain Nolan said. "We'll look for the *Gulf Storm.*"

The captain returned to the radio, where he gave orders to his boats to search to the north, while the helicopter flew south. Everybody on board scanned the sea. A shrimp boat hove into sight and the copter flew low over her. But it was not the *Gulf Storm*.

"Perhaps she docked somewhere south of Port Canaveral," Pete suggested. Captain Nolan thought this was a possibility and ordered his pilot to fly low over the coast line.

Many coves and inlets came into view below the noisy copter. People beneath them in sailboats and cruisers looked up, astonished.

Finally the pilot beckoned to the captain and pointed dead ahead. The mast of a shrimp boat could be seen making for a secluded inlet ringed with palm trees and palmettos. As the helicopter drew closer, Pete and Pam saw four men on the deck.

"One's Ferguson! And there's Turk!" Pete cried.

"Right," Shorty agreed. "They're heading for that small dock."

By carefully maneuvering the copter over the tree-tops, the pilot landed the craft just as the *Gulf Storm* drew alongside the dock and Ferguson jumped off.

Captain Nolan leaped from the aircraft, followed by the others. "Halt!" he called. "You're under arrest. All of you."

"What for?" Ferguson said angrily. "Just because the Hollister kids don't like us?"

"Where's the lost nose cone?" the officer asked sternly.

"We don't have it," Turk said. "Search our boat if you like. We can prove that these young meddlers are all wrong about us."

While the pilot stood guard over the crew, Captain Nolan, Uncle Walt, Pete, Pam, and Shorty searched the *Gulf Storm*. In the cabin they found a powerful radio and depth-finder equipment, more modern than Shorty had ever seen on any shrimp boat before.

A good catch of shrimp lay in the ice chest, but there was no sign of the missing missile pay load.

"Let's look under the nets," the captain said. Shorty probed the huge pile of gear but found nothing.

"What did I tell you!" Ferguson shouted triumphantly.

"Wait!" Pete cried. "What's this?" He pointed to a thin, strong wire cable fastened to the side of the *Gulf Storm*. It disappeared under the water and came up on the opposite side.

All the fishermen paled at Pete's discovery. Turk started to run away, but the pilot quickly grabbed him by the collar. "What are you hiding under the boat?" he demanded. The men looked from one to another, but said nothing.

"I'll swim down and look, sir," Pete volunteered. He quickly stripped to his shorts and dived over the side. Quickly he swam beneath the *Gulf Storm*. Seconds later he reappeared.

"It's here! The nose cone!" he shouted.

"Good work, Pete," Captain Nolan said. He turned to the prisoners. "Now you can talk, because your case is hopeless."

Uncle Walt wrung Pete's hand and hugged Pam. "You'll never make a bigger catch than this. Will they, Shorty?"

The fisherman grinned and danced a little jig. "Not in a thousand years," he declared.

While Captain Nolan guarded the sullen crewmen, the pilot radioed for help and soon the speedy launches arrived. The four prisoners were handcuffed and taken aboard the helicopter, while crewmen from the launches stood guard over the precious cargo lashed to the bottom of the *Gulf Storm*.

Pete dived in to look under the boat.

"We'll get experts from Cape Canaveral to carry the cone back," Uncle Walt said and gave directions by radio.

On the way back to the port, Captain Nolan questioned Ferguson, Turk, and their men. The two ringleaders would not talk, but the other men, named Cooper and Allen, poured forth a torrent of information to keep from getting a maximum sentence.

Ferguson and Turk, they said, were not really shrimp fishermen. They were shrewd adventurers who had rented the *Gulf Storm* and signed up two hands to look for missile debris.

"Dale Ferguson convinced us we wouldn't get caught," Cooper complained.

"Who's he?" Pete asked.

"The phony who calls himself Bittley. He's Alec's brother."

Cooper and Allen said that the nose cone would have been sold to the highest bidder, either in this country or out of it.

"Turk figured the parts alone would be worth a fortune," Allen said.

"Thanks to the Hollister family, your scheme didn't work," Uncle Walt said.

Cooper glumly admitted that the myna bird and the monkey that Turk had found added to their undoing.

"Where did the bird learn missile talk?" Pete asked.

"From Ferguson and Turk," Allen said, jerking

his thumb toward the ringleaders. "They know lots about missiles; even worked for a while on West Coast launchings."

"But why did you take the monkey?" Pam asked.

"Ha, ha, that was a big joke on 'the brains,'" Cooper said, looking at Ferguson. "He wanted to offer the monkey to the laboratory at Patrick, just so he could get inside and pick up information about the lost nose cone. Dale got in as Bittley and drew a rough sketch."

Pete snapped his fingers. "That explains the sketch of the lab building!" he declared.

"When you kids got suspicious, Ferguson let the monkey go that night on the beach," Cooper finished.

Back at Cape Canaveral, the prisoners were taken to jail. Pete, Pam, and their uncle returned home.

"Hurray for the heroes!" Aunt Carol said as they entered the house.

Pete's face flushed as Ricky, Randy, Holly, Sharon, and Sue plied them with questions. "We're not heroes," he said. "All of us helped solve the mystery."

"That's right," Mrs. Hollister said. "Marshall Holt, and even Lady Rhesus has a share in it too."

Sue ran into her bedroom and returned with the monkey seated on her shoulder. Lady was dressed in a space man's suit. "Mommy and I made it," the little girl said, her eyes twinkling.

Just then the telephone rang. Uncle Walt answered. "It's for you, Pete."

The boy took the phone. "Oh, hello, Marsh. . . . What? How did you find out? . . . Okay. Good-by."

Pete ran to the television and turned it on. A newscast had started, and the announcer, looking straight at the children said, "The Hollister and Davis children have solved the mystery at Missile Town, along with their friend, Marshall Holt."

"Oh, goody!" Holly shrieked.

"Sh-sh!" Pam said, pulling one of her sister's pigtails.

The TV announcer went on, "As a reward for their fine detective work, the Air Force will take the children on a special tour of Cape Canaveral tomorrow."

"Yikes!"

"Crickets!"

"The President of the United States also will tour the base tomorrow," the announcer added, "and will shake hands personally with each of the children."

Shrieks of happiness filled the room. When the tumult had quieted down, Sue said, "Now listen to my words." She held Lady Rhesus on her shoulder and Missy in her arms.

"We're listening," Pete said, laughing.

With a roguish shake of her head, Sue declared, "I told you we'd meet the President."